THE OFFICERS' WARD

THE OFFICERS' WARD

Marc Dugain

Translated by Howard Curtis

Originally published in this translation by Phoenix House,
the Orion Publishing Group Ltd, London, 2000

First published in the United States in 2001 by
Soho Press, Inc.
853 Broadway
New York, NY 10003

Library of Congress Cataloging-in-Publication Data

Dugain, Marc.
[Chambre des officiers. English]
The officers' ward / Marc Dugain ; translated by Howard Curtis.
p. cm.
ISBN 1-56947-265-3 (alk. paper)
I. Curtis, Howard, 1949– II. Title.

PQ2664.U3475 C4313 2001
843'.914—dc21
2001020558

10   9   8   7   6   5   4   3   2

For Eugène Fournier

I KNEW nothing of the Great War. I knew nothing of the muddy trenches, the dampness that seeps into the bones, the big black rats in their winter fur dodging among the mounds of refuse, the stench – a mixture of cheap tobacco and half-buried excrement – and over everything, the unvaried metal-grey sky that unleashes a torrent of rain at regular intervals, as if God can never refrain from hounding the ordinary soldier.

Of that war, I knew nothing.

I left my village in the Dordogne on the day of mobilization. My grandfather covered my escape from the family home in the stillness of early morning. I wanted to avoid an emotional scene, which would have been pointless. I loaded my kit in old André's cart. With his brown mare swinging her rump in front of us, we headed for Lalinde. It was only when I got off at the station that he said to me: 'Don't be away too long, my boy – it's going to be a great year for wild mushrooms.'

In Lalinde, there were a dozen young men, all with moustaches, all dressed up in their new tunics, as if in their Sunday best, letting themselves be embraced by mothers with red, tear-stained faces. As I watched old

André disappear into the distance, a big round-faced boy with eyes like marbles came shyly towards me.

It was Chabrol, from Clermont-de-Beauregard. I hadn't seen him since elementary school. He was on his own – no family, no farewell – and he was apprehensive. He had never travelled by train before, and he was afraid of missing his connections. To steady his nerves, he kept sipping from a flask attached to his belt. It was a mixture of plum brandy and Monbazillac. He had three litres of it in his bag, one litre for each week of war – he'd heard the Germans would be on the run within three weeks. The smell of the mixture hung about his big body like the smell of some strange communion wine. He sat down next to me and wouldn't take his eyes off me. The little train stirred itself, and we set off for Libourne, where we changed to a Paris train. Once in the capital, we had to change trains again, to reach the Gare de l'Est. The station was dense with people. The commotion was deafening – shouts, weeping, the strident whistling of the locomotives. We reached the barrier, beyond which no civilian was allowed to pass, and I pointed out Chabrol's train to him. He took my hand, and shook it, unsteadily, reluctant to let go.

'Well, goodbye, Adrien, see you soon. Thanks for the company. Maybe we'll see each other at the front.'

'If not at the front, then in the village, Chabrol. And take care. Don't try to be a hero.'

'Oh, there's no chance of that, I can tell you. No chance of that at all!'

I waved to him one last time from a distance before he

was engulfed in the tide of people sweeping towards the trains.

I pushed and shoved my way through the crowd, having more than once to extricate my kitbag from between a father discreetly hiding his feelings and a mother timidly waving her handkerchief.

I was bathed in sweat. It trickled between my legs and my woollen trousers, making me itch. I decided to rest for a moment and relieve myself of my kitbag, which was chafing my shoulder.

When I looked up, I saw a woman in tears, holding the hand of a frail young man in a tight-fitting uniform who was trying to keep his balance on the steps of the train as everyone jostled him in their hurry to get on. I took out my packet of tobacco. The doors of the train closed. The young woman waved to the conscript, who was already gone, swallowed up in the rush. As she stood there on the platform, I could find nothing better to do than to speak to her.

'Don't be upset. It'll all be over in a few weeks.'

She did not reply.

'Was that your husband?'

She looked at me for the first time. She had a sad, beautiful face. 'No, a friend.'

'Which section is he in?' I had to shout to make myself heard.

'The infantry, like everyone else.' And she added, more out of politeness than genuine interest: 'What about you?'

'The Engineers. I'd say that was obvious, wouldn't you?'

She allowed herself a brief smile at my joke. Then she took a step forward, and I had the feeling I was going to lose her forever.

'I can take a later train,' I said hastily. 'I know it's not done, but I'd like to invite you for a drink. There is a war on, after all!'

She agreed, though her mind seemed elsewhere.

I felt as if I had turned into a blind person's guide dog. Weighed down with sorrow, the woman followed me on unsteady feet. We sat down on the terrace of a large café opposite the station, and gradually she came back to life. I remembered the soldier's face, his drooping moustache, the tunic that hung loosely on his sunken shoulders. The woman and I sat side by side, facing the frenzied traffic on the avenue. I did not dare look at her properly. I had the sense that something was beginning, and I felt nervous.

She stared straight ahead, apparently oblivious to the crowds passing to and fro. From time to time, she would pick up her glass, take a sip, and immediately put it down again. We did not say much. I learned only that she was a musician, that her name was Clémence, that the soldier was a composer, a friend of Debussy, Fauré and a whole swarm of famous musicians whose existence I had never suspected, that she lived in Montmartre and mixed in artistic circles, that she was friendly with the Norwegian painter Edvard Munch, that her future parents-in-law were as stupid as they were generous, and that she hated the countryside.

After that, my own story was less impressive. I was an insignificant railway engineer, specializing in bridges and tunnels – though even that was a major step up from my blacksmith grandfather and my father who had been steward of an estate belonging to the Water Board. I had always lived in the countryside or in little provincial towns. I had only begun to work in Paris in May, and had barely had time to get to know the city before war broke out.

There was a little more sparkle in her eyes as she asked me if anybody would be waiting for me when I returned from the war. I replied that I had no ties. She was surprised. She suspected me of being a Don Juan – I looked the part, she said.

How could I explain to her that all I knew of love was the vague feelings I had had for the girls in the higher classes at school? Or that I had had very few women? The first was called Ernestine Maillol – but what did the name matter? She was the daughter of the district notary, a caricature of the irascible bourgeois. It was with her that I had learned about women, in a barn on the estate where my father worked.

I had had brief relationships with other women after that, relationships that were sometimes tender but never passionate. To judge by the fleeting glances that were occasionally thrown my way, women genuinely seemed to find me attractive. But there was no hurry – I had many years before me in which to seduce and love all the women I wanted.

Clémence then began to talk about the war. A monstrosity, she said, loudly enough for everyone to hear. It was clear she intended to shock, and I had to keep smiling in an attempt to placate the people at the neighbouring tables, who looked as if they were about to intervene to put a stop to the scandal. And as she was a woman, it was obvious that I would be the one they would tear to pieces. I preferred to leave that pleasure to the Germans.

She was on the verge of tears. Now she was blaming God – it was faith that incited men to wage war. 'If it wasn't for that damned belief in eternal life,' she said, 'men wouldn't go so confidently to the slaughter!'

I had been educated for two years at a Jesuit school, at the instigation of my mother, who was a believer – unlike my father, whose one principle in life was never to disagree with his wife. While there, I had quickly become part of a small group that upheld pagan values, particularly the gathering of wild mushrooms when the chestnut trees were in blossom. We had a stepladder to help us get over the wall during school hours, and to use it we had to give a password. To the question: 'Who is God?' we had to answer 'God is a little fellow without a tail.' In my opinion, it was doing God a great honour to hold Him responsible for this war. The only ones responsible were the Germans, and I had no reason to think otherwise.

The louder Clémence talked, the more vulnerable she

seemed. She was desperate for her pianist's hands to be saved. Just one bone of one finger – he only needed to lose one bone for his life to be ruined. Not an arm, a leg, an eye, just one little bone.

She suddenly stopped talking, as if her mechanism had wound down.

'And now, what are you going to do?' she asked, after a silence.

'I don't know. Probably go back to the apartment I have here, and catch a train for the Ardennes about five. There's no shortage of trains today. I haven't slept at home for a week. I was in the Dordogne for my grandmother's funeral. And what about you? What are you doing?'

'I have nothing planned. I'm going home, that's all.'

'Clémence, forgive me if I ask you a stupid question. I promise it'll be the last. This friend of yours – this pianist – do you love him? Obviously, you're under no obligation to answer.'

'Of course I love him. But perhaps you'd like me to answer the question you haven't asked me?'

She could sense how embarrassed I was. I had never had to deal with complex emotions before. It was something new, something disturbing and at the same time rather intoxicating.

'The thing you're really wondering,' she went on, 'is: "What about me?" Well – what about you?'

'My answer, which you're free to forget the moment I say it, is that this war may last a few weeks, perhaps even a few months, and in all that time I'll be surrounded by

7

men. The only woman I'm likely to meet will be leaning over my stretcher, trying to stop the bleeding. It would be nice to think that I could spend these last few hours with you. With all due respect to your prior commitments, of course.'

Her blue eyes wandered absently over the animated crowds for a moment. I was very afraid that she was about to stand up and leave me high and dry. But she simply said: 'Take me home with you!'

I hailed a cab and we left.

Clémence was my idea of a modern woman. I wasn't very sure what a modern woman was, but if such creatures existed, Clémence was surely one of them. None of the women I had known had ever behaved like this.

Clémence inspected my little apartment in the rue de Milan as if it might reveal all the things she had not been able to find out or guess about me. Even the cast-iron stove took on an importance I had never before suspected.

She looked through my piles of books. All I had were technical books about bridge and tunnel construction. A few books on military history, too, but a pitiful lack of anything on art or literature, or anything that might connect to her world of artists and free spirits.

I was struck by the contrast between my damp, gloomy lair and Clémence's proud bearing. A pair of socks and some broken braces, strewn on the dusty wooden floor, mocked me from a corner of the room.

'I haven't been here for several weeks,' I said,

indulgently. 'The place is a bit run down. I'm afraid it's not likely to get any better.'

A large sitting room, a small bedroom, a shower, a tiny kitchen – it wasn't exactly the ideal setting for what awaited us. But that did not seem to matter to her.

The question she asked next surprised and embarrassed me.

'Don't you find that fear increases desire until it's unbearable?'

'I think I shall be in a better position to answer you in a few weeks' time,' I replied, trying to imitate her detached and casual manner, 'but I doubt it's the thing that's uppermost in the mind of someone who feels the cold steel of a bayonet against his throat.'

'You know perfectly well I'm not talking about physical fear. I mean that vague but intense inner fear, the kind you can't shake off, that suddenly seizes hold of you and then vanishes as quickly as it came.'

'That's not the kind of fear people talk much about in my village. I imagine city folk are more susceptible to it.'

I would have been lying if I had told her that the desire I felt for her derived from any kind of metaphysical fear, or even from my anxiety before going off to war. Men of the soil know that they are mere links in a chain, a chain governed by simple laws. To delve any deeper is to torture yourself for nothing. City folk are the centre of a world they have created for themselves. They are tormented by inner doubt, and worry themselves to death over it.

★

Time was pressing. Silence had descended on Paris. I had to catch the first train, at four forty-five in the morning. Any later, and I would be considered a deserter. I tore myself from the damp sheets and groped for the constituent parts of my uniform, which lay scattered like the pieces of a jigsaw puzzle. A beam of light from the street lamp outside fell across the room and came to rest on Clémence's white body. I tried to wake her, to whisper something in her ear, but she was fast asleep.

I went into the next room, found a piece of paper that was big enough for her to see when she awoke, and scribbled a few words.

Clémence, I have to go. I leave you the apartment – you can stay here as long as you like. When you go, please drop the keys in the letter box, and above all, leave your address in Paris for me to find when I return. I am going now. I just want you to know how much you have begun to mean to me. Take care.

I kissed her one last time, on the base of the neck, and went off to war.

If my kitbag had not been so heavy, I would have jumped for joy in the street, hopping from foot to foot like a little boy who has just found a rare coin in the gutter and thinks it will last him his whole life through.

IT was autumn. The weather was beautiful, warm and balmy, the air limpid. It felt like the first day at school. We were quartered near a village in the Meuse, not far from the river. Soldier were flooding into the camp, brought in on carts pulled by requisitioned draught horses. Eighteen-year-old kids in red and blue, their eyes bleary with sleep from their night on the train, all of them so industrious, so eager to do things well. The camp was a hive of activity – horses harnessed and unharnessed, tons of merchandise loaded and unloaded, provisions, covers, tents, girders, planks. The sixth regiment of Engineers was getting down to work. We might have been on full manoeuvres. There was an air of determination about everyone.

But all I really wanted to do was sleep. Looking at the branches of the trees in the warm, hazy air and seeing the leaves move in the morning breeze, I found myself daydreaming. In the fragile tranquillity of that pre-war day, scattered images mingled in no particular order. I thought of Clémence, my new love, a love so brief but so intense that it worried me as much as it delighted me. I thought of my father, struck down barely two years before, at the age of forty-seven, by a cancer that had grown on his liver without causing any pain until it was the size of a melon – killed while he was revelling in the success of his son, an engineer and an officer. The family was rising a little higher with each generation, in both knowledge and social standing, and this century was promising to be better than ever. All we had to do was recover Alsace and Lorraine. I thought of my younger sister, who was so fond of me – I was eight years older than her and she listened to me as if I were her father. I thought of my mother, her mind like a larder, her lack of substance revealed for all to see since my father's death – my father who had protected her, all the while deceiving her on his regular Thursday rides to the market in Bergerac, when he would take the opportunity to visit a lady, no longer very young, who lived behind the church and of whom it was said that she lifted men's moustaches for a few francs.

And I thought of my grandfather, whose last glance as I departed had spoken volumes about his fear of the Prussians, a hangover from the defeat of '70, of which he still kept an indelible mark in the form of a blow struck from behind by an uhlan's lance. At the meal after my grandmother's funeral, when the saddler had asserted that the Germans would be sent packing in a few days, my grandfather had replied: 'You remind me of the story of the joker who bets his pals he can swallow three big flat stones. The pals come back an hour later. "How far have you got?" they ask. The joker replies: "There's only one left." Then he lowers his eyes and adds: "Plus the two I've got in my mouth."'

To my grandfather, the Germans were those stones.

'S-s-sir!'

The excited little fellow with the bulging eyes pulling me roughly out of my drowsy reverie was Chabert, the chief warrant officer of my platoon. A career soldier, bent like a croissant, whose anxiety to do his duty brought him out in a stammer.

'S-s-sir, the captain wishes to see you in – in his quarters.'

The captain was a huge, portly fellow. A pleasant enough chap, but there was something political in his friendliness – he liked you as long as you did what he wanted, and as long as you didn't put him in a difficult position with his superiors, but when problems started he would leave you to fall with the same affable smile.

'Look here, Fournier, the reason I've called for you is that I've been looking through your file and your service record, and I see you're a real expert in mobile bridges.'

'You could say that, sir.'

'Engineer in Applied Arts, three years of military service in the Engineers, a few precious months' experience in civil engineering. I don't suppose you're related in any way to the Fournier who used to work in the Civil Engineering department and is now a colonel on the general staff – your father, perhaps?'

'I'm afraid not, captain. My father is dead.'

I sensed his disappointment.

'Actually, Fournier, I have a mission for you. I want you to take charge of a detachment and search for the most suitable spots to place mobile bridges over the Meuse.'

'When must we leave, sir?'

'The earlier the better. The Germans are getting closer. We expect them on the opposite bank tomorrow, the day after tomorrow at the latest. We're staying in this position for the moment – always ready for the offensive, of course. I'm counting on you, Fournier.'

Then a vague look came into his eyes, as if he found it difficult to hide his anxiety.

'Tomorrow at dawn. You and two sub-lieutenants. That should be enough to get the lie of the land.'

He opened his drawer and took out a bottle of *marc*, probably requisitioned from an abandoned farm.

'Would you care for a drop, Lieutenant?'

With the war not even started yet, he was already scared. I found myself taking my first swig at nine o'clock in the morning. Leaving the captain's quarters and crossing the village square towards my platoon, I heard shouts, and saw men running in all directions. Chabert was jumping up and down like a demon.

'What's all this commotion, Chabert?'

'S-s-sir, s-s-something terrible . . .' He paused to catch his breath. 'The horses, sir . . .'

I advanced, cutting through the privates, who were running about in panic.

One of my boys was lying on the ground, half disembowelled, his head supported by two of his comrades.

'God almighty, what happened?'

'S-s-sir, it was an Ardennes horse, ungelded,' Chabert explained. He had practically shrunk to half his former size. 'A kick, sir.'

'And what idiot had the bright idea of bringing a stallion here? Since when do we requisition horses that weigh a ton without cutting their balls off?'

I approached the lad. A thread of blood was running from his ear to his neck.

This was the first man killed in my platoon, a peasant boy disembowelled by an Ardennes horse. His eyes glazed over, and his head fell to one side, his lips half open. I took off my helmet and observed a few seconds' silence. Then I asked Chabert to go and fetch the regimental chaplain. I was sure the peasant boy was a Catholic.

The first day of school was over.

I woke at dawn. The camp was asleep. In forty-five minutes, reveille would sound, but for the moment nothing moved. The only noise came from the thick canvas of the supply tents flapping in the morning breeze. I walked unhurriedly to the stables, which were housed in the outbuildings of a presbytery.

In the half-light all you could see were the rumps of horses, horses of every type – chestnuts, mackerel greys, blacks, bays. There were half-breeds, saddle horses, draught horses – anything we'd been able to requisition from the neighbouring farms and manor houses in forty-eight hours. The grooms had been notified the night before. Everything was ready. The saddle and the provision bag had been laid out on a makeshift trestle. My horse had been curried and brushed down in the early hours of the morning. He was a brown bay. Three of his legs had white stockings, and the edges of his eyes were unpigmented, which gave him a roguish look. The two second lieutenants arrived, in full dress uniform.

I wondered which platoon the captain had dug these two up from. I hoped they'd at least stay upright in the saddle. I already had one man dead. I reminded them we were on a reconnaissance mission, not a stag hunt. We had a good fifteen kilometres to ride, and I thought it would be a good idea to try and be back by midday. The Germans were not very far now from the other bank.

We followed a towpath that ran alongside the Meuse. The sun had emerged from behind a layer of silver clouds, and the day was warming up. In the distance, a church bell struck seven. I had known hundred of mornings like this with my father and grandfather – the damp soil smelling of moss and mushrooms, the light through the leaves, the still morning landscape, the only sounds the noise of the horses' hooves and the jingle of their harnesses. The two second lieutenants followed, tangled up in their reins, their feet barely in their stirrups. One shot, and they would be bent low over their mounts.

My mind wandered, and I let it drift. I imagined Clémence by my side, lying against me on the river bank. It was as if she had taken up residence inside me. I should have talked to her more. It was too late now. There was so much to tell her when I returned.

Although I didn't believe in God, what I did believe was that each of us has a guiding star, and I counted on mine. Some men meet their deaths earlier than others, and I believed that a man who thought about death postponed it. As if you could keep the enemy at bay by talking to him, being constantly on the watch for him. I remembered an old woman who lived in Liorac, a healer. People came to consult her from far and wide. Her cures were as effective as her bad smell. She prided herself on her gifts of clairvoyance and always told those who consulted her that their fates depended on which of their dead watched over them. And as she knew everyone within a radius of twenty kilometres, she felt sorry for those she knew whose ancestors had met violent deaths. I had long been convinced that the one who was watching over me was my great-grandfather, who had died at the age of ninety-eight while opening a second bottle of Péncharmant as consolation for having decided the day before to give up smoking. With such a forebear, I could not possibly die in the war.

We were approaching the bank. My two men were talking. I gestured to them to be quiet. This was the place where the Meuse narrowed, and this was where the front-line troops would have to cross, this evening or the next day. I would make notes and take measurements. I searched in my saddle holster for a notebook and a pencil. Where were my binoculars? My horse had been trotting so unevenly that my bladder was full to bursting. I dismounted and settled down against a birch tree.

There was a loud bang from somewhere close by, and

for a split second a whistling sound. I just had time to see a head severed from its body, the body itself bending at the knees, the horse collapsing. The other officer, who had remained in the saddle, slumped in my direction, his shoulder blown away, the bone sticking out like a shank of ham. I felt as if an axe had embedded itself just under my nose. Then the light went out.

THE spider spins its web. Slowly. Sure of what it's doing. It's the natural order. The spider waits for the fly. The fly is caught in the web. The fly has lost. It doesn't complain. There is no tragedy in nature.

The final futile efforts of a fly – that was the first image I saw when I regained consciousness. A fly hanging from the ceiling above me. The ceiling was white and cracked and the paint was peeling.

A second image replaced the fly – the lower chins and the tips of the moustaches of two men deep in conversation, their arms crossed, who glanced at me from time to time without seeing me. I caught, as if from a distance, snatches of what I guessed was a conversation between an officer and a surgeon.

'They'll give him the Legion of Honour, while there's still time. What's your diagnosis?'

'I fear gaseous gangrene, Captain. It's six days since they found him. Apparently he'd been lying there at death's door for at least two days. They brought him in this morning. They didn't dare touch him while he was in the ambulance. He's definitely the first casualty of this type we've had. His wounds are a swamp of pus. The cavity is full of purulent matter. The only reason he didn't bleed to death was that the mud thrown up by the shell stopped the lingual artery from haemorrhaging. Unfortunate for him – without that, his sufferings would have been over by now.'

'So what do you think about the Legion of Honour?'

'There's still time, captain.'

I gathered together my remaining reserves of strength and grabbed the officer's sleeve. I tried to utter a few words, but nothing came. So I made a gesture with my hand to indicate 'no', pointing to the place where medals are usually pinned. I saw a surprised look on his face, before I lapsed back into unconsciousness.

I was woken a few hours later by a pain so strong and so diffuse that it was impossible to know exactly where it originated. My feet were moving. Both of them. My hands, too. Both my eyes pierced the semi-darkness. I was whole. With my tongue I felt around my mouth. At the bottom, it pressed against the gums of the lower jaw – the teeth had been pulverized. The top part, though, seemed to stretch away like an endless corridor. My tongue encountered no obstacle, and when it reached the sinuses, I decided to cut short my first visit. It was all that emptiness that was causing the pain.

Again, I saw two chins moving above me. Two men in white coats. Again I tried to speak, but all that came out was a dull gargle like the moaning of a big mammal.

The doctors had not noticed my unfortunate attempt and continued to hold forth about my case. I couldn't move my hands and feet, which were tied to the camp bed with two long straps. There was a lot of movement in the corridor, which resembled a marshalling yard. It was obvious the war had well and truly started. I had not been the victim of a mere warning shot across the bows.

'They filled in a form at the first-aid post, but you can't read it, there's so much saliva and blood on it.'

'Let's have a look. Severe maxillofacial damage. Look at this, old man! Everything open from the top of the chin to halfway up the nose. Upper maxilla and plate both completely gone. Space between mouth and sinuses no longer compartmentalized. Tongue partially gone. Organs at the back of the throat unprotected and visible. General infection of the tissues because of all the pus.

'Now let's enumerate the problems!' he continued. 'Risk of gangrene through infection of the wounded parts. Risk of infection of the airways and pulmonary regions because of the lack of protection. Risk of anaemia owing to the difficulty of feeding the patient through the mouth or nose. Conclusion, Charpot – get the poor blighter out of here and behind the lines. Val de Grâce is the place to take him. As far as I know, that's the only place they might be able to do something for him. If gangrene doesn't set in. In the meantime, clean the wounds. Arrange for him to be transported by train. Don't take him by river, that's too slow. Try to feed him once before he leaves, by nasal probe. Keep the straps on. Especially if he's conscious while being fed. It could be painful.'

'Anything else, Major?'

'Nothing else, Charpot. In the meantime, don't leave

him here. His wounds stink too much. Anyone still standing is likely to drop just at the smell of him.'

I stayed like that for hours, gradually losing the strange lucidity I had had when I first woke up. I had a recurring dream. I was chewing a large ball of clay and staring, from underneath, at a series of bottles that glittered as they turned. The fever was spreading through my joints like a dull fire. It weighed on the base of my skull, pressing me into the bed. The bed was made of thick stretched canvas, but what remained of my senses was so affected by my wounds that it seemed as soft as down.

I no longer knew where I was. I seemed to feel the presence of death, prowling restlessly. Behind the opaque curtain of my delirium, I could sense movement. In the distance, I heard a stretcher bearer calling a nurse:

'We're changing his billet for the night. The idiots have only just noticed he's an officer. Which means we can't leave him in the general ward for his last night at the front.'

Early in the morning, a nurse leaned over me and examined my face. She had big sea-blue eyes, and a slight down covered her chin. Another one interested in me without really seeing me. When she finally realized I existed, she spoke to me. From the intensity of the look I gave her, she must have realized I was trying to ask her something.

'I'm going to feed you, Lieutenant. You'll see, it's good soup.'

She was talking to me the way the two nuns used to

talk to my old aunt, sitting shrivelled in her armchair near the window, as they tried to unlock her jaws, old gates rusted by years of neglect.

To tell the truth the taste of the soup worried me less than the way she was going to go about getting it in. The answer was not long in coming.

My first conscious meal was served to me through a rubber tube topped with a little receptacle that contained the soup. When the receptacle was raised, the soup went down. And vice versa. Simple physics.

'We're going to put it in your nose. Stop breathing through your nose and just breathe through your mouth.'

She was treating me like someone who was simple-minded. I suppose it was because I was dribbling. A man who dribbles is obviously simple.

The soup entered through my sinuses. I choked and struggled. The nurse hit me on the back. My stomach retracted, and I hiccoughed. And we started all over again.

Six stretchers were lined up at the front entrance of the country hospital. For some reason, they had finally decided against the sanitary wagon. We were to be taken to Paris by ambulance. Three bunks on each side, one above the other, for six seriously wounded men. And two stretcher bearers to take turns driving. It would take at least twelve hours to reach Paris. They put me in the bottom bunk on the left, behind the driver. I didn't have the strength to sit up and see who my travelling companions were. The one opposite me couldn't have been more than eighteen. He had the profile of an angel. His eyes were closed. His covers followed the outline of his body down as far as the base of his knees, then fell away sharply.

The ambulance started up, and with it the groans of my comrades. The infantry sergeant above me – I could see his stripes on a sleeve that hung down from his bunk – sobbed like a little boy and begged for his mother.

For the next few hours, my only view was the linen cloth of the bunk above me, and a bloodstain that grew larger as the hours went by, like ink on a blotting pad.

The pain in my sinuses returned and spread through all the tissues of my face. I found myself thinking about opium, the opium that travellers talked about. It might loosen the pincers that held my mouth tight. The concert of groans gradually faded, as if each man were leaving the choir in turn to sink into darkness. The stretches of cobbled road were torture.

The young fair-haired soldier lay motionless, his face livid. He had not woken since the beginning of the journey. He reminded me of a pen portrait of L'Aiglon on his deathbed, which I had seen in my grandfather's house, in a nineteenth-century edition of *Le Magasin pittoresque*.

After several hours, the ambulance stopped in the courtyard of a hospital. We couldn't have arrived yet. The doors of the ambulance opened to let a doctor get in. He gave the six patients a cursory examination.

'Take these two out,' he said, pointing. 'They're dead. We've got two others for you.'

We changed drivers the way they used to replace horses on the old mail coaches. L'Aiglon was taken away, his body as stiff as a statue, so stiff they had difficulty getting it out of the ambulance. Then it was the turn of my neighbour overhead – the bunk had soaked up what remained of his blood. The two substitutes were loaded on and we set off again. My new neighbour tried to talk to me.

'Hey, you, any idea where we're going?'

I tried to reply. Nothing came out but bubbles of air, as if I were chewing soap. Not a single sound. Resigned, he settled into his corner and launched into a long monologue.

It was getting hotter. I felt cramps in my face, as if each muscle were tightening, then it all became transformed into a huge toothache, with each nerve playing its part in the score.

My new neighbour continued his soliloquy. He was talking to his mother, telling her about his war. He was afraid she would scold him. He kept telling her he had done nothing wrong, and that the Germans had thrown a shell at his legs.

The ambulance rattled over the cobbles, the suspension rods creaking interminably. If I had not been strapped in, I would have been on the floor. With all the sweating and dribbling I was doing, I felt thirsty. The thirst became so obsessive that I wondered if pain were not preferable.

The ambulance stopped in open country. The doors

opened, letting the mild air of late afternoon rush in. The two ambulance men stood there, pulling faces.

'God almighty, what a stench!'

I couldn't smell anything. I realized something I had not been aware of up until then – I had lost my sense of smell. The air wafting in from the meadows gave me a vague sensation of coolness, but not the slightest scent of the late summer afternoon.

The two big canvas flasks the men were holding brought me back to my main obsession of the moment. They squirted water into the mouths of the other five patients, but when my turn came, the ambulance man grimaced and called his acolyte.

'Hey, we're not equipped to give this one a drink.'

'It may not even be advisable. If we do something stupid, we'll never hear the end of it. Leave it, he'll last till tonight.'

The doors closed again, and the convoy set off once more.

The engine was getting noisier and noisier, making me fear the worst – a night in open country without a drink. Finally, I dozed off on my bunk, the rising fever numbing my pains but making me even drier.

When I woke, rain was drumming on the roof of the ambulance. The fact that we were going slowly, and constantly changing direction, made me think we'd arrived in a town. A last row of cobbles, the crackling of gravel, then we came to a halt. The doors opened. We were taken out one after the other. I tried to open my mouth to catch the big raindrops as they fell. You never knew, maybe I would have to wait for the opinion of the resident doctor before I got a drink. And I couldn't say anything. Even if I could, I had nothing to say.

THE ward reserved for officers was as vast as a station waiting room. A high, rectangular ceiling, white and cracked. Ten or so lattice windows looking out on a yard which was where I supposed the convalescents took their walks. It was a little early for convalescents. The first casualties were only just starting to arrive. As it was a long way from the front here, this was where the most serious cases were brought.

The iron beds had been carefully aligned facing the windows, away from draughts. Everything was in place, every detail had been meticulously worked out – it was clear they were expecting a lot of patients. The covers were neatly folded, the bedpans carefully placed under the beds.

The whole floor had been set aside for officers with facial wounds, but I was the first to arrive. The empty beds would gradually fill with men who as yet knew nothing of what awaited them. Their fates still hung in the balance. A leg, an arm, a shell blowing up in the stomach, the head – or just a few weeks' reprieve?

The men who were going to join me would have memories of combat, hand-to-hand fighting, great offensives, whereas I had been cut down without ever having been under fire. I had never even seen the enemy face to face, and would never be able to tell my children what a German looked like. I would have to invent the big moustaches and the pointed helmets.

In those early days of September, it was the sense of being defeated without having fought, the absurdity of my fate, and my powerlessness before it, that caused me more suffering than my facial wounds.

My head was wrapped in bandages. Only my mouth and eyes were visible. But I suppose that was enough to give my face some kind of expression.

There was a worker doing something above the beds. As he and I were alone in this station waiting room, he spoke to me. He was a man who was too old to fight and too young to do nothing.

'It's started the same way it did in 'seventy. We're retreating. They say the Germans'll be in Paris within ten days. It's a bad situation and no mistake. I say: That's the way it is. You have to have fire in your belly, otherwise it's a complete disaster. But those Boches really fixed you up good and proper, didn't they? And where did they do that to you? In the Ardennes? Can't you talk? God, they must have really hacked you about for you to be brought here! Even if you can't talk, I guess you can listen. I was talking to the ward sister yesterday. Not the hard little one with the hairy chin – she's not a sister – but the plump one who talks nicely to everyone. She said they're expecting tons of patients, and from what she was saying, they're only going to put the ones who've had their faces messed about in your ward. Just disfigured officers, she said. They've done the same for the privates downstairs, and it's already filling up. But you're the first officer. You're lucky. That way you get to choose your bed. That's why they asked me to take down all the mirrors – because of the kind of customers they're expecting. Well, that's understandable, there could be some nasty surprises otherwise. But the bars on the windows are nothing to do with me, they were already there.

'They really sorted you out,' he continued, unscrewing his last mirror, 'but you've come to the right place. For a start, it's clean. And then there are some real prizes among the nurses. You're a hero, too – it's easier for people like you. And as nobody can see what's behind those bandages, the little tarts imagine what they want. Anyway, I'll be off now, I just hope they don't have to evacuate you down south. But anyway, in the state you're in, you have nothing more to fear. See you again, mister officer, sir.'

The missing mirrors had left a large rectangular shadow above each bed.

The nurse came in first, head down, a determined look on her face. Then the doctor, a tall but rather stooped fellow in his forties, with a decisive manner. In three strides, he was by my bed.

'Good day to you, Lieutenant. Not feeling too lonely, I hope? I'm afraid you'll soon have some companions. Tonight perhaps, or tomorrow at the latest. Not suffering too much?'

He did not wait for a reply, which I could not give him anyway.

'Not the type to complain, eh? Good! Now this is the plan. We're going to feed you. You have to build up your blood and bones. Trust me, we're bang up to date here. In two or three days, we'll operate – put things back in a bit of order. Then rest, a lot of rest, before we really get down to business. It'll all take time, of course, but you have plenty of time. Not in too much of a hurry to get back to the front, I suppose?

'But if the war does drag on,' he continued, as if to encourage me, 'and you do have a chance to get back there, it'll certainly be with a brand new face. I even guarantee your moustache will grow back. I'll be along to see you every morning. We'll give you a slate and chalk for writing, until you're able to talk.

'You're lucky, you know,' he went on, in a confidential tone. 'The face is a bit alarming, but there are no complications. Very good vascular capillarity. No gangrene, contrary to what the old school used to think. You've only two things to worry about – breathing well and eating well. The rest is up to me.'

He turned to the nurse.

'Let's see,' he said, in a loud voice. 'Monday today. Make sure he eats three times a day until tomorrow night. I need him to have an empty stomach on Wednesday morning – the operation's at six. If he's really in too much pain, give him a little morphine. Just as long as he doesn't get used to it. We won't have enough for everyone, if they keep streaming in like this. I'll see you soon, Lieutenant.'

The nurse had the amiable expression of those who devote their lives to others. She sat me up in bed.

'I'm going to feed you.'

She came back a few minutes later, carrying a big wooden tray, which she placed at the side of my bed. There was a bowl of steaming soup, a white plate full of little pieces of shrivelled meat, and a pair of tongs. The nurse poured the soup into a container shaped like a duck's head. With the tongs, she crushed the little pieces of meat and mixed them into the soup. She placed the duck's beak in my mouth and poured the mixture. Which of us looked more like a duck, I wondered – the instrument, or me? I had a premonition that this tiresome exercise would become a constant ritual, and that I would never again eat without a duck or tongs.

The nurse came back to see me as I was trying my best to get my stomach used to working on its own. She spoke loudly, as if I were deaf on top of everything else.

'I've brought you a slate and a piece of chalk, in case you have anything to tell me, and some paper and pencil to write to your family. You must let them know where you are.'

I only had four small sheets, so I could not afford any false starts. All I wanted was to put time and distance between my family and me. I wanted them to ignore me, not even think about me, much less worry about me.

I therefore set about composing a letter that would be

even more reassuring than if I were at the front, between two battles.

My dear mother, my dear grandfather, my dear sisters.

I am writing to you from Paris, from the Val-de-Grâce hospital to be precise. I was wounded by a German shell while on reconnaissance. Nothing serious. No vital parts hit, not the eyes, the legs or the arms, just the collarbone damaged. A piece of good news for all of you – I'm not going back to the front. I eat well here, the nurses look after me, I'm living like a lord. I have to stay several more weeks to avoid complications. This is not a good time for you to come north. Stay where you are. I'll come down as soon as I can. Things are in a bit of a panic and the wounded are pouring in. That's why visitors are not authorized. Tell my uncle Chaumontel not to come, it would be pointless right now.

So you can rest assured. For me, the war is over. I did my duty, that's what matters. I'll write to you as often as I can. If you don't receive anything for several weeks, put it down to the mail, for I assure you, now that I'm here, nothing can happen to me any more.

Finishing the letter, I had the feeling I had gained a little time, and I caught myself hoping the war would go on for quite a while longer yet.

I still had three sheets. They were for Alain Bonnard, my oldest friend. From primary school to military service, we had always been together – until now. Bonnard had been born with a small right hand, and the fingers were still no bigger than those of a child of eight. He would certainly have been able to hide his handicap more easily if people didn't always hold out their right hand. As often happens with those who feel diminished in some way, Bonnard had compensated for his infirmity with a superior intelligence, and the only reason he had not tried to enter the Ecole Polytechnique was that he knew I would never get in and he had not wanted to go there without me. I knew that to him I represented a degree of physical accomplishment which he would gladly have traded with me, even if it meant also acquiring my weaker brain. Bonnard was a perfect example of the success of the Republic's educational system, which had allowed the son of a café owner in the Périgord to become an engineer, and it caused him a great deal of anguish that the recruiting board had not allowed him to give back to the Republic what he felt he owed it. He would never wear the officer's uniform to which he was entitled. Instead, he had been assigned to a minor desk job in an arms factory.

In my letter, I told him simply that I had been wounded in the head, and that although my life was not in danger, there would probably be a long period of convalescence, which was why I was asking him to bring me a pack of cards and some books – I left the choice to him, having, as he well knew, no particular literary tastes. I informed him of my wish that he should remain the only one of my acquaintances in Paris, or even back home, to know my whereabouts.

Three more sessions with the duck and the tongs, and I was nearly ready for my operation. Nothing much happened during that day and a half, apart from the doctor's announcement that the War Minister would soon be paying a visit to the wounded, including me.

I had been fast asleep for several hours that night, when I became vaguely aware, in the background of my dreams, of movement in the ward. New patients were being brought in.

At dawn, I was taken to the operating theatre and given ether to put me to sleep.

When I woke up a few hours later, I felt very sick, and my face was plagued with constant, nagging pains, like pins and needles.

They had taken off the bandages so that the blood from the wounds should not soak through, and my wrists were tied to the bed with straps to prevent me infecting the scars in my half-conscious state. Everything was black around me. They had placed a dome-shaped frame above my head, the kind conscientious gardeners use to protect young plants, and the whole thing was covered in thick canvas, leaving me in complete darkness.

I didn't regain full consciousness until the afternoon of the following day, when, with the screen removed from my face, I opened my eyes to the light and saw two other men, each in a corner of the ward, both lying completely still, one of them groaning weakly.

That was the moment Bonnard chose to enter the ward, his right hand in his pocket. I was surprised he had been given permission to see me, and I imagined it was because I was still receiving special treatment – that would stop as numbers increased and I became just one of the anonymous mass. I was the first man he saw, but he looked away and approached the other two, peering into their faces. Then he stopped and turned back to me. I could see the horror in his eyes. He seemed about to leave – perhaps he hoped he had got the wrong ward – when I made a little gesture with my hand. As he walked uneasily towards me, I clumsily picked up my school-boy's slate and chalk, and wrote in big letters: *'It's me, old chap.'*

He sat down on the edge of the bed, took my hand and began to cry. We had never been particularly demonstrative with each other, but now he was power-less to prevent the flood of tears that submerged him. As if to distract my attention, he began to take some things from a small shopping bag – a pack of cards, some old books, a bar of chocolate and a packet of tobacco. The last two he immediately put back.

'Is there anything else you need?'

I shook my head and picked up my slate.

'Could you do me one last service?'

'Of course,' he replied, eagerly. 'You know you can count on me.'

'A woman left an envelope in my letter box. Could you fetch it for me?'

'Where's the key?'

'The concierge has it. Tell her it's for me.'

'I'll see it to it, Adrien, I'll see to it. Don't worry.'

I could sense how deeply upset he was. By the horror

of the sight, of course – although it was difficult for me to imagine what he was seeing – but above all by the way in which our relationship had changed. His little child's hand must seem very trivial now. I sensed that he was in a hurry to bring this first visit to an end. He had been through a lot of strong and confusing emotions in a short space of time. Before leaving, he shook my hand one last time between both of his.

'You're a hero, Adrien,' he stammered, 'a true hero. I'll be back to see you soon.'

The following day, I got up for the first time. As I was unsteady on my feet, I kept close to the iron bedsteads, like an early navigator not straying far from the coast. With every step I took, I was afraid I would collapse, but my curiosity was greater than my fear.

When finally I reached my goal, I bent over one of the two new arrivals. He lay on his back, a little crucifix in his right hand, held tight against his chest. He had no bandages, and his face was exposed. His chin was gone, blown off by a shell, I assumed. The jaw had yielded like a dyke hit by a tidal wave. His left cheek had caved in and his eyehole was like a looted bird's nest. He was breathing gently. I went on my way, pausing at each empty bed until I reached the third occupant of the ward.

His ashen complexion and black hair contrasted with the whiteness of his pillow. His profile was flat. The missile had blown away his nose, leaving his sinuses gaping, and the absence of an upper lip gave him an inquisitive grimace. I understood why our ward was filling so slowly, and why we were on the top floor. In this big room without mirrors, we became each other's mirror.

My doctor came in first, followed by the resident and two staff officers who ushered in the War Minister. Of the three of us in the ward, I was the only one conscious. The doctor introduced me briefly to the minister.

'Lieutenant Fournier of the Engineers, Minister, wounded in the Meuse in the very first hours of fighting!'

'Lieutenant Fournier,' the minister said, 'I am here to express to you our country's gratitude for your bravery and your sacrifice. Without men like you, the land of our forefathers, which we must hand on to our children, would be under the sway of German barbarism. We are proud of you!' He shook my hand. 'Where are you from, Lieutenant?'

'He can't talk yet, Minister,' the doctor cut in quickly.

One of the staff officers stepped forward. 'Don't worry, your words have been noted down for the press, Minister.'

'Very good, very good. Be brave, Lieutenant. They tell me you'll be back on your feet in a few weeks and ready to return to the front. We need men like you. Goodbye, Lieutenant.'

The minister left the ward with his entourage. Despite the noise, my two companions did not wake up.

I had not quite grasped what had just happened, and yet it had made me feel really proud.

THE patient with the ashen complexion died that morning. The shell had damaged his brain so badly, he hadn't stood a chance. A few minutes after the nurse had finished her first round, they came to take him away – hurriedly, as if to obliterate all trace of him.

A new casualty came to take his place a few hours later. As I had been in the ward the longest, the nurse made it her duty to inform me of the comings and goings.

That was how I discovered that the newcomer was a pilot whose plane had gone down in flames over the plains of the Marne. So the Germans had got as far as the Marne! He was still wearing his aviator's jacket and boots, a uniform that arouses admiration in every infantryman. But his face, which I could only glimpse in the half-light coming from the window that looked down on his bed, was like a big black toffee, burned and deformed. No trace of a moustache or eyelids. Nothing that could be called human.

When the surgeon came for his daily visit, he told me that my first operation had been a success, and that he had managed to overcome all the constriction that had resulted from the tearing of the tissues. Because of the trust he had in me as an officer, he said, he was being honest with me. He went on to explain in detail the further operations I would have to undergo.

'The truth is, Lieutenant, I am waiting for material to reconstruct your upper jaw, and in particular, your palate, which as you know, is missing. The only method we can possibly use is a bone graft. We need the bones of a child who has recently died. I've informed my colleagues in the civilian hospitals of the urgent nature of my request. As soon as one of them can provide the raw material, if you'll pardon the expression, I'll be able to press ahead with the reconstruction of your upper jaw. Of course, it'll take more than one operation, but we're on the right track.'

When darkness fell, the ward with its high ceiling was silent as usual. I dreaded the restless nights, the oppressive nightmares that woke me at regular intervals and that always began again where they had left off, before I fell back to sleep, cradled by the dull moaning of my companions, who clung to life without being aware of it.

But waking up and having to face reality was even more terrifying.

The only thing that managed to revive my sense of smell was ether – only to send it to sleep again immediately. And taste, which is said to come from the palate, had been forever obliterated by the soup of ground vegetables they forced down me day after day. I had the feeling that my whole personality revolved now around this gaping hole that nothing could fill. The only thing that can grow again after it has fallen is a stag's antlers. They were talking about joining my lower lip to my nose, but it was impossible to imagine how they could give any kind of form to such rags and tatters.

I dreamed about Clémence every night. During the day, I forbade myself to think of her or relive the memories I had of her, let alone imagine her future. The thing that distinguishes man from the animals is that animals have no thought for the future. In my case, that would have been a blessing. Not that the present brought much relief either.

I had no taste as yet for reading other people's stories, for following the threads of their lives, with mine still so chaotic. While my companions fought to regain consciousness, I played cards, alone. My grandfather had taught me to play patience. From time to time, I would pause in my game – I always won – to observe the others. In the silence of the great ward, I would sit and watch their chests rising and falling in rhythm with their breathing.

It had been dark for several hours when the surgeon entered the ward, alone and moving more slowly than usual. He pulled up a stool, sat down, leaned over me and rapidly examined my wounds.

'We're making progress, Fournier, we're making progress. You're out of danger. I think you suspected that, didn't you? But we still have that hole to deal with. What concerns me is how to stem the constant flow of saliva. Pulling the skin to remake the upper lip is nothing. The hardest thing is to get the cartilage grafts to take, so that we have something solid to support the skin. You were lucky in one respect. Your tongue is practically intact. You have everything you need to speak, but in order for what you say to be audible, we have to be able to channel the sound. At the moment, there's nothing to stop it going off in all directions. But we'll get there, you'll see.'

He looked round the ward.

'Not many here yet. If you could see the privates' wards – they're full to bursting. The first ward has forty-eight beds, and they're all taken. None of the surgeons can remember anything like it. Especially the facial wounds. It's because of the artillery. The Boches don't like chucking anything small at us. But medicine is advancing, we're making great strides. By the time the war is over, we'll be able to make faces as good as new, as if nothing had happened. Progress out of carnage – what a paradox, eh? Well, I must be off, I'm operating at five in the morning. I did fourteen operations today, and no two were the same. There are so many different cases, I wonder if we'll ever be able to classify them all. Legs and arms are simple, we just cut them off. Sometimes higher up, sometimes lower down, but all we have to do is cut them off. With maxillofacial cases, it's not a question of amputation, but reconstruction. That's what makes it so fascinating. More for us than for you, I admit. Anyway, this time I'm finally going to bed.'

He gave me a friendly little pat on the arm as he stood up, and went off to have a quick look at my companions. As he left the room, he let out a great sigh.

44

It was already late. I had decided to get up. I wasn't feeling well. I felt cold inside. I pulled a cover off one of the many unoccupied beds, wrapped myself in it like an American Indian, and set off down the corridor towards the lights of the street. There, at the window, it was easy enough to find an angle between the profound darkness of the hospital and the light of the street lamps where the glass reflected my image. I was in what was known as a 'drying out' phase, and wasn't wearing any bandages, so that what I saw was the image of a man with a tunnel in the middle of his face, a tunnel whose edges were irregular and torn. The image, unreal and yet true, did not affect me. To my surprise, I felt no desire to cry, in fact I was not troubled at all. To my even greater surprise, my stomach heaved and I found myself emptying its entire contents over the borrowed bedcover. It felt like another defeat – and certainly not the last.

Bonnard came in after the early afternoon treatment session. He seemed just as upset as before, and anxious to find some detail that would prove to him that this really was his friend he was seeing. He approached on tiptoe, for fear of waking the other men, whose return to consciousness was expected at any moment, and handed me a letter.

'This is all I found in your box.'

I opened the envelope. I did not want to attach too much importance to the letter, although it was my last link with the world. With my other hand, I squeezed

Bonnard's forearm as if I were on the edge of the precipice. And I read:

Dear Adrien,

The moment I stole with you seemed to me all too brief, but delightfully intense. I surrendered to those deep eyes of yours, which give your perfect face such an impression of strength. I'm sure it was the mad atmosphere of that day of mobilization that made us both surrender. You know I am committed to another man, and you know, too, how much he needs me. To see each other again would be madness. We must not build anything on the basis of a physical attraction we both share but which has no future. It would be too cruel of you to hold this against me.

Forgive me, therefore, if I do not give you my address, or if I leave it to chance whether or not we ever see each other again. I shall never forget the face that bewitched me. Thank you for leaving me to get on with my duty.

Your sincere and devoted
Clémence

I folded the letter carefully and placed it on my little bedside table. I picked up my schoolboy's slate and chalk and wrote:

'*Thanks for taking the trouble. It was an important letter. Tell me about yourself. What are you up to?*'

'I've been assigned to the research department of Bachelot and Roy, an arms factory making cannon shafts. I feel as if I'm useful, as if I'm participating in the war effort. Of course, my name won't appear in the history books, children won't read about me at school, but I'm doing what I can to help my country. Do you get any news from the front?'

I indicated 'no' with my forefinger.

'It was a close-run thing. The Germans had pushed us as far as the banks of the Marne before we finally managed to drive them back. They were that close to Paris. We're on the offensive again now, but I'm afraid the war's going to last longer than we thought at first. If it's not all over by winter, we'll have to wait at least until spring, or even summer.'

It was Sunday. Bonnard spent the rest of the afternoon sitting by my bedside. I didn't suggest we take a little stroll. I didn't have the courage to face other people's eyes, even the eyes of cripples – it was still too early. So Bonnard was condemned to talk to me the whole afternoon. And his skill in the difficult art of the monologue showed me once again how keen a mind he had, and how good a friend he was.

I remembered how much he liked painting. I had caught a glimpse of his gifts whenever he left a drawing or a watercolour lying around in his room at boarding school. I knew how strong a passion it was from the fact that he used his little hand for painting – he had forced himself to write with his left hand. He talked to me about his masters, the Cubists, a school that, in his view, could not help but reflect the violence of the times. He told me that he himself was trying to give his work greater expressiveness and that when the war was over there would be a profound upheaval in the art of painting.

He left me as night fell, without ever having really talked about himself. He promised to return the following Sunday.

Once the last nurse had passed, the lights went out one by one. I had brought up my meal. My stomach was weary of doing all the work, without any support from my teeth. My saliva glands were working overtime, producing vast quantities of foam. I had no sense of improvement. I was on the steady road to decline. I was waiting for a child to be torn from the arms of its parents in order for them to rebuild my upper jaw. The woman I had expected to revive me had driven another nail in my coffin with her letter, and we were going to lose the war – Bonnard was hiding it from me to spare my feelings.

I got up and groped my way to the cupboard where my military things were being stored until I was finally declared unfit for service. My pistol was there, in its holster. An administrative error – it should have been given up. I felt the heavy grip. The bullets were in the belt. I took three and inserted them very carefully in the barrel. Three bullets for three good reasons to die. I pressed the barrel under my ear, the only place on my head that did not hurt.

It was a strange sensation to be at my own mercy. It was one of those moments when you see things clearly, and what I saw clearly was the extent to which life depends on the fear of death.

It wasn't the image of my mother, or my sister, or my grandfather, that prevented me from pulling the trigger –

it was simply the thought that I would be finishing a job the Germans had started.

I finally put the pistol away again where I had found it. I made a lot of noise closing the cupboard in the hope that my companions would at last wake up.

The service now occupied five wards. On the first floor, two wards for the privates. On the second floor, a ward for subalterns with facial wounds. On the third, a ward for disfigured subalterns and, at the end of the corridor, a smaller ward for commanding officers – with only one occupant so far, a colonel.

The first of my two companions to regain consciousness was the one with the little silver crucifix in his closed hand. He was a cavalry captain who had fallen in a morning offensive in the Argonne. 'Henri de Penanster' was the name written on the card hanging on the bars of his bed. It sounded like a Breton name. Half his chin had been blown away by a shell, which had also torn the carotid artery in passing. While Penanster lay on the ground after this first wound, a horse falling dead from an enemy bullet had kicked him in the face with its hoof, puncturing his eyeball and smashing the eye socket. He would certainly have bled to death like a rabbit if the mud had not stemmed the blood pouring from his open carotid. Still conscious and thinking he was done for, he had begged a young front-line nurse for a cross. She had taken off the one that hung around her neck. He had clasped it in his hand and had not let go of it since, even when he was completely unconscious.

Before he had fully recovered consciousness, they put a kind of vice in his mouth to counteract the constriction of the jaws. Every day, a nurse measured how wide his mouth had opened, and noted it carefully on a sheet of paper hanging at the foot of his bed.

Pierre Weil, the pilot with burns, was covered with fatty matter on the face and hands. When he had been hit, his engine had burst into flames, burning his hands and face except where the goggles protected his eyes.

But fate had not yet done with him. His plane had crash-landed against a tree, and he had been flung out of the cockpit, saving him from the fire but smashing his face.

When you came down to it, only the dead could envy us. And I wasn't even sure about that.

Clémence was in the background of all my thoughts. The feeling of betrayal engendered by her letter had only turned me against her for a few days. I knew I would see her again, even if it took months or years. I would see her fade, I would see time blur her figure and make inroads into her beauty. But I, with my mutilated face, would never age. The war had made me an old man at twenty-four. I had not had the courage to kill myself. I had had the courage not to kill myself. Bitterness and rancour threatened. I was confronting the enemy within.

The leaves on the bushes in the convalescents' yard were the colour of autumn now. Covered in frost, they were beginning to fall. The war was settling in for the winter, and everyone was digging in. Bonnard was right. Bonnard was often right. New lodgers had joined the ward of silence. Nobody spoke. We might have been in a library, everyone studying and observing silence for the sake of the others. The boldest launched into monologues – most often at night – but the sound that emerged was scarcely louder than the sound of water boiling. Some of the arrivals were young, others less young. What did it matter any more? Their wounds had smoothed out the differences.

All ten beds were occupied now. The ward was full. Penanster and Weil had been given the beds on either side of mine. Penanster was taking his first steps, though still hanging on to the bars of his bed. They had taken off the vice, which had not given the hoped-for results. The wooden pincer that had replaced it had proved equally disappointing. They had finally plumped for a sack of coal, which was fastened to his lower jaw with cords. Every afternoon he spent an hour standing with his back to the wall. A strap tied around his forehead kept his head against the wall and stopped it from falling forward under the weight of the sack of coal that was pulling his jaw down. The whole procedure took place in a room they called the torture chamber, a terrifying place full of diabolical machines, where the patients underwent exercises to overcome the problems of constriction. The results were soon apparent. His mouth opened a centimetre and a half in seven weeks. Another three years, and he would be in a position to open his mouth as wide as La Fontaine's crow its beak.

Penanster said his prayers in the dark, morning and

night. I wondered what on earth he could possibly say to God and how he could speak to Him without anger.

Weil's head looked like a prehistoric skull. His sinuses were exposed, and his lower lip was thick, giving him a sullen air. But he knew how to laugh with his eyes. The smoke of the blazing plane had burned his bronchial tubes and vocal cords, but I knew he would be the first to talk again. And something told me we wouldn't regret it.

With all the new arrivals, the number of nurses had been increased. I was surprised to note that they were getting younger and prettier.

I supposed it was an attempt to bring a little brightness into the lives of the severely wounded patients and soothe their troubled hearts. With the aid of my slate and my chalk, I asked my accomplice, the ward sister, who took care of me as if I were a newborn baby.

'The truth is,' she whispered in my ear while the others were taking their afternoon nap, 'they put the youngest ones on your floor because downstairs they were shamelessly flirting with the patients. Well, you can imagine, all the men off at the war, months without male companionship . . . The upshot was that things started happening that shouldn't. When the senior doctor found out, he lost his temper and decided to send all the young nurses to the maxillofacial floor. "They won't be tempted there!" he said.'

When the early cold of winter had gripped the little courtyard, the doctor informed me that a maternity hospital in Paris had been good enough to send him the body of a stillborn infant. The main parts of the skeleton had been removed and, he specified, not without a certain satisfaction, coated in petroleum jelly and stored in a refrigerator.

'We now have everything we need for your operation. We're going to operate on you at dawn. It'll be a long operation. As far as I know, it's a first in the field – the graft of an upper jaw. Obviously, we have to count on two or three months for the graft to take.'

Endlessly, I made the same calculations. Three months for the upper jaw. Then three months for the palate. If everything went as planned, in six months I would be talking. Another six months to draw the curtain on all that, to close the upper lip and the cheeks, and I would be back outside.

They came for me in the early hours of the morning, when all was quiet, and sleep had finally overcome even those who were most in pain. I had had a literature teacher at school, who had been very fond of Greek mythology, and had often told us the story of Sisyphus. It had not meant much to me as a schoolboy, but now, on the eve of every new operation, the myth of the man rolling his stone up the hill came back to me. The form of the punishment had changed, and its severity, but after all it had to match the new means of destruction we possessed.

Once again I entered the ether fumes and came out of them with my head crushed in a vice, which was loosened day by day, and then it started all over again. The longer the war went on, the more wounded there were, and the lower the doses of morphine after the operations, the more we suffered and the less we spoke about it – otherwise, we would have spoken of nothing else. Operation followed operation, digging deep into tissue and nerve, until the body wearied of these constant assaults – and all for the sake of results which, even when you could see them, looked more like crude plastering jobs than plastic surgery. People were sent home with their faces vaguely patched up, like a series of veal escalopes sewn together, and the only thing that showed clearly that their faces were not upside down was the position of the eyes. Luckily, we were beginning to get in supplies of head bandages. There were black ones, white ones, bandages for the right or left eye, and half-face bandages which were identical whether it was the lower part of the face that had to be covered or the area from the upper lip to to the forehead. The standard bandage had no eyeholes. Most of those who had been hit in the top half of their faces had left their eyeballs on the battlefield. The lucky ones simply had to cut out one or two holes the size of a large coin. There was plenty of time for that.

The usual sign of a return to life after an operation was a return to the gambling table – in fact, just a stool. That was where we played *belote*. And the good news was that Weil was starting to talk again. With a voice that sounded as if it came from beyond the grave, but at least he was the first of us to emerge from his silence.

The bad news was that they were trying to reconstruct his nose with a skin graft. The graft was nothing in itself, what counted was the method. The one they had decided to use was the Italian method.

They fix the patient's wrist to the top of his skull with a metal splint or a plaster, so that his biceps are in contact with his nose. Then they make an incision in the skin of the biceps and make sure it adheres to the nose, and wait for the graft to take and the skin to revive by itself. That position, with the biceps on the nose, day and night, can last weeks or even months, however long it takes for the little piece of skin to adhere to the costal cartilage grafted underneath. It is not a new method. Apparently, it was already being used two centuries after Christ to remake broken noses. It has the grave disadvantage of immobilizing your hand, making it impossible to play cards. Not to mention having your arm in the middle of your face, taking up most of your field of vision. Or the muscular pains caused by the discomfort of the position, or the pins and needles in the numb arm, which deprived Weil of sleep even when the pain of his other wounds gave him a little respite.

At night, when he lay in bed, the triangle formed by his harnessed arm looked in silhouette like the sail of a Breton schooner returning to port over an oily sea.

But Weil was categorical. 'I want a nose,' he said. 'Not a little nose, a proper Jewish nose.'

Weil was a man immune from doubt. I was still not sure how much in his personality was just bravado, but he did a great deal of good to the whole ward. He assured us that before the week was out he would have the little red-headed nurse who collected the bedpans in the morning, working on the principle that charm had nothing to do with looks, and that it was precisely his ugliness she would fall for.

A week later, he had to admit defeat.

'She doesn't find me ugly enough,' he concluded. 'But I did what I could.'

His graft was to prove a failure. The new nose began to decay, because the skin was too charred and weak to receive it. Weil had to be content for a while with a cardboard nose that looked like the top half of a bird's beak. After that, they tried a whole range of plastic noses on the same model, until they finally fitted a permanent prosthesis. This was a nose from a child's doll, the material of which was closer in colour and flexibility to human skin, although its smoothness was quite a contrast to the rest of his permanently swollen face with its patchwork of variegated hues in a range between blood and charcoal.

Among those who joined us at the beginning of that winter of '14, two died without ever regaining consciousness. Both had sustained injuries to the skull.

At the end of January '15, a very young infantry lieutenant was brought into our ward. He had smashed his jaw by firing a pistol under his chin. The bullet had ploughed an impressive vertical trench through his face before exiting via the nose, but the brain had not been hit.

He was put in the bed to the left of Penanster's. It was rumoured that he had tried to commit suicide in the face of the enemy, a theory which the trajectory of the bullet appeared to confirm. To me, and to my comrades, that counted as an act of treason.

For Penanster, who was a Catholic, it was even more unforgivable. He asked in writing that the lieutenant be moved to another ward. But there was no room anywhere else. The card games resumed, with all of us turning our backs on him.

I received two letters a week from my family, and I wrote them one. There existed a sort of convention between us that we would never talk about what really mattered, but only about things of minor importance. My letters were like those a child writes from a holiday camp, carefully avoiding any mention of the emotions, good or bad, aroused by living in a group, just concentrating on eating, drinking and sleeping. All my letters respected the same order of priorities. Their one aim to keep my family at a distance, to put it to sleep.

My mother regularly drew up lists of the local boys who were missing – Lacassagne, Vigeac, Louradour, Despiesse, and the Castelbujas brothers.

When we were children, the Castelbujas boys' mother worried constantly about the things that might happen to her two sons. They could be trampled by horses' hooves or bitten by snakes, they could climb a tree and fall. Everything we did together was potentially tragic. Whenever Bonnard and I walked the two brothers back to their house, she would be waiting for us on her doorstep, her eyes brimming with tears, and always uttered a set phrase that had us laughing in advance:

'My poor children, how worried I've been!'

I was not too bothered by the fact that they were missing. As long as they kept their wits about them, they were sure to find their way back in the end.

Having asked Bonnard to make inquiries, I learned that Chabrol had died three weeks after the start of the conflict. Probably when he had nothing left in his flask.

My sister Pauline's letters were longer, and I could sense that she was genuinely worried. I knew that she was the one who had sent the Chaumontels, our cousins from Nogent-sur-Marne, on a reconnaissance to the hospital. I had them turned away with the excuse that I was receiving treatment at the time. I expected her to appear any day now. I was almost grateful to the Germans for bombing Paris and keeping potential visitors away. My grandfather had simply added a few words at the end of one of Pauline's letters: 'Good show, my boy. You're a credit to your country and your family.'

My bone graft didn't take. The surgeon assured me he had not said his last word. I, of course, was no nearer saying my first.

One day, as the nurse who had rejected Weil's advances was passing my bed, I stopped her and showed her my slate. She waited patiently while I wrote:

'Would you like to see something you won't see with any other man?'

Seeing that I was holding my sheet tight around my waist with my other hand, her face turned as red as a beetroot. I stared into her eyes.

And stuck my tongue out at her through my nose. Even Penanster smiled at that with his one good eye. The little nurse turned tail and ran.

For the first time, I made a complete circuit of the floor. As I walked alone along the circular corridor, I passed nurses I knew, who were used to the way I looked. But there were others who could not bear to look me in the face.

I reached the windows that looked out on the boulevard de Port-Royal. Trams, carriages, a few cars, a man striding along with a young elegant blonde woman on his arm, a young man in a hurry twirling his cane, a governess frantically running to catch up with the children in her charge. A group of young people patting each other on the back. Life was going on, like a faint hum that even the noise from the front could not drown.

So it was still possible to be twenty, not to be in the war, to be whole. The people outside were not my people. I felt more comfortable here, among my comrades. I crept back to the ward, my head spinning from the fresh air of the corridor.

The surgeon was convinced that a second graft was necessary. The lower jaw was moving again. All that was needed now was something to support the tongue at the top, something to take the place of the palate, and I would be able to talk again.

The external wounds were all healing well. The nurse took me to the room where they made facial moulds. Why did they need to make a mould of my face? I had no idea, and didn't want to know.

When I entered the room, I was seized with terror. Some thirty disfigured faces hung from the wall, like the trophies of a warrior tribe. This parade of deformity, neatly displayed on the white walls, was too much for me. I recoiled like a horse frightened by ghosts, and ran back to the ward, where Penanster and Weil were waiting for me to make up a fourth at *belote*. They had opened our window wide. The air that came in was still and warm – autumn was taking its time.

There was a letter from my mother on my bed. I was always afraid she might have learned the truth. But it was the usual kind of letter. She asked how they were feeding me, and recommended me to eat cheese to build up my bones. At the end, she added that they had found the two Castelbujas brothers, one two days after the other. Both dead.

I had been the first patient in the ward. In thirteen months, I had seen a large number of comrades pass through. Some had left as silently as they had arrived. Others, mended as well as they could be, had rejoined their families. They had all supported us and had promised to write and tell us what had changed outside, and they had all done so.

We had spent a year in this ward, occasionally venturing timidly as far as the circular corridor.

No music had reached our ears except the music of pain.

We had swallowed 785 bowls of soup mixed with

chopped-up meat, and only ether had been able to revive our resigned sense of smell.

We had spoken to each other in a language of strange facial movements, like fish.

We had met a large number of pretty young women who knew nothing of us but our sessions on the bedpan and the fetid smell of our internal injuries and the simian expressions of our deformed features, our faces fixed in grotesque grins, as if laughing even when our pain was at its most extreme.

Some had blamed God for choosing them as living testimonies to how easily a man's identity could be destroyed, while others had turned to Him to save their souls from the shipwreck. We had all cursed the Germans and had all been convinced of how useful we were.

THE days went by, every day the same despite our efforts to enliven our little community. It was like a monk's life, with an extra dose of suffering, and without the spiritual enlightenment. There was the same renunciation, the same rigid and unchanging rhythms that were both soothing and oppressive. The mental life of a war casualty, condemned by his wounds to spend months on end in a military hospital, revolves around a small number of recurring thoughts, which are seldom profound and which others would certainly find obsessive. The first task was to eliminate from our consciousness anything that might remind us that our former lives had been organized, as are most people's lives, around our senses. The second was to forbid ourselves to think about the future except in terms of the small daily advances we made in the chewing of food and the uttering of words.

Well before we began talking to each other, an intense bond had formed between Penanster, Weil and me. The day finally arrived when, the foundations having been judged sufficiently solid, I was given a prosthesis, a piece of rubber to take the place of my palate and separate as best it could my mouth and my sinuses. The air was at last able to circulate normally, and my tongue had a support to help it utter its first intelligible words. Long weeks went by before it was finally fixed. Sometimes, at night, the rubber collapsed, obstructing my breathing. Tired of being suffocated at such an awkward time, I would spit out the apparatus, and it would end up on one side of my bed or the other. In the morning, I would go back to the treatment room, where they would put it back and make me promise to stop my 'target practice'.

That little piece of rubber helped me greatly with the palatal consonants, the *t*'s and *d*'s, and provided an enclosed cavity for all the other sounds which up until then had disappeared at the top. The letter *s* reappeared in my conversation a few months later, when they fixed a dental apparatus to the upper and lower jaws. Just when everything seemed to be going well, they took out the palate because it was infecting the skin, and advised me to use it only for long conversations and put it away the rest of the time.

That created a strange formality in my relations with my comrades. I was particularly fond of having long talks with a bridge engineer, who was completely deaf in his right ear and had to use an ear trumpet to hear with his left one. Whenever one or other of us decided to begin a discussion of any length, he would alert me by pointing a finger at his mouth. I would then insert my imitation palate and he his trumpet, and we would talk with an intensity rare among those to whom speech comes easily.

Weil, despite real difficulties in diction, was the only one of us who was not sparing with his words. He made it his business to brighten up our days with little

64

comments on anything and everything. Penanster's pronunciation had returned to something close to normal, but it wasn't in his nature to take advantage, and he continued to count his words as if he only felt himself to be in possession of a limited number of them.

I have often wondered since what exactly it was that drew the three of us together – a Jewish aviator, a deeply devout Breton aristocrat, and a secular Republican from the Dordogne. It wasn't our enforced proximity. That could just as easily have made us hate each other. Our wounds, of course, brought us closer, and the two others were always there to accompany whichever of us was on his way to the operating table and to rally round him as soon as he returned. But we felt the same solidarity with the other men in our ward, as well as the limbless patients on the ground floor.

No, what brought us together right from the beginning was a tacit decision to reject introspection and avoid thinking about the disaster of our existence, because that would only lead to bitterness, a bitterness made up in part of disenchantment and in part of a martyr's selfishness.

CURIOUS as ever, Weil had taken to exploring the corridors, and had discovered that near the ward intended for commanding officers, which was still not full – it had only three occupants – there was a little room no bigger than a broom cupboard. From the corridor where we took our daily stroll, we could see the nurses going furtively in and out. This secretive game had been going on several months before Weil discovered that there was a woman living in the little room.

One evening early in the summer of 1916, she appeared in the corridor. A beam of light from outside shone on her beautiful hair. She had a slender figure. She stood motionless for a few moments, looking out of the window, with her back to us. When she made up her mind to go back to her room, she turned in our direction, and we knew then that she was one of us.

That evening, we were in a subdued mood as we sat down at our gambling stool. Penanster left the game earlier than usual, and Weil went to bed without saying a word, which wasn't like him.

I often recall that forehead and those perfectly shaped blue eyes, looking out gloomily from the remains of a face disfigured by a man–made war.

After that evening, she did not reappear. I assumed she had chosen a different time for her surreptitious forays into the corridor overlooking the boulevard de Port-Royal.

The woman's presence disturbed us greatly, although none of us let on to the others quite how much. We had been fighting this war for the sakes of our women and children, and to find a woman here among us in the hospital had a doubly negative effect on us – we had failed in our mission, and we were powerless to punish the enemy who had dragged us into this war.

We knew that a joint approach from the three of us would frighten her, just as any move that seemed even slightly official, such as via the nurses, risked leading to her removal.

We agreed to delegate Penanster, thinking him still quite distinguished-looking, despite his mutilated face. His wounds were no less severe than ours, but his left profile was almost intact, and still gave some indication of what he had been before his disfigurement – something we noted with envy.

We were sure our wounds would frighten the woman, like mirrors reflecting her own misfortune, but when, after days of waiting and watching, she came out and found herself face to face with Penanster, she did not shy away in the least.

'We are forming an officers' club,' he explained. 'So far, there are three active members, all of them voluntary benefactors. We have noticed that there is a lack of women. Would you like to join?'

Her only response was to give us a warm and immaculate smile. Her mouth had been totally spared, as had her eyes and her forehead. She was like a bed of roses from which the flowers in the middle had been uprooted. She had been hit in the nose and the cheekbones, and the explosion had also punctured her eardrums. As Penanster carried on talking, she continued to smile, with the smile of those who live in a world apart.

Penanster realized then that she was deaf and could only read his lips. He alone had an intact mouth, in which words formed definite shapes. I realized at once that neither Weil nor I could ever talk to her – the sounds of the reconstructed words we formed would never reach her ears, and the movements of our lips were meaningless.

Continuing to communicate with her in the same vein, Penanster expressed surprise at her presence among us. In a mild, soft voice that made her wound seem all the more unjust, she told us her story. We listened in astonishment, leaning on each other for support, quite abashed by this admirable woman whose charm seemed unaffected.

Towards the end of 1915, there had been a shortage of nurses, and Marguerite had volunteered. At that time, she had been as beautiful as she was useless. Her father was a silversmith, quite comfortably off, and she had had no lack of suitors, all either shirkers or rejected as unfit, but she dreamed of falling in love with a brave man. She was assigned at first to a hospital behind the lines, where her beauty caused so much disturbance, among both patients and doctors, that the situation quickly became untenable. Probably without any idea of what the reality would be like, she persuaded an officer she had previously rejected to send her to an emergency unit at the front.

Marguerite had never been afraid, but in her first two days at the front she had wept a lot, and even vomited, at the sight of the torrent of casualties with their severed limbs and slit throats and eviscerated stomachs. On the third day, a scathing reprimand from the doctor in charge dried her tears. On the fourth day, while they were trying to stop the bleeding from a leg cut off in mid-thigh, and she was passing the instruments – there was no longer time to clean them between one patient and the next – a German shell fell on the tent.

The blast carried off both the wounded and their carers. Everyone was killed – except Marguerite, who was left disfigured and deaf.

Marguerite naturally became our chief concern from that day on. To talk to her, we would first address ourselves to Penanster, who would then repeat our words to her, enunciating each syllable slowly and clearly. As is often the case with deaf people, she was afraid of talking too loudly, and we never tired of listening to that soft voice – such a marked contrast to the groaning sounds we produced. She very quickly became part of our clan, even though our daily meetings were always brief.

She had not informed the members of her family of her condition. She never wrote to them. When they finally tracked her down, she refused to show herself. Penanster was dispatched to tell them that Marguerite had no wish to receive them. When her father, getting up on his high horse, asked the reason for this refusal, Penanster replied that he didn't know it. He sensed that the two brothers were relieved, especially the more robust of the two, clearly a shirker and looking well on it, in contrast to his sibling, a chalky-faced youth who never stopped coughing. Penanster could not take his one good eye off the face of Marguerite's mother, staring at her so insistently that she became embarrassed. She was not to know that through her features Penanster was trying to reconstruct her daughter's face, to get some idea of a structure that was now gone forever. He found the mother's face similarly well proportioned, but quite lacking in the gentleness that gave Marguerite's face a glow which even her wound could not diminish. The encounter over, Penanster bowed and turned his back on that family of bourgeois from the *grands boulevards*, straight out of some mediocre drawing-room comedy – a comedy that in the end was more sad than funny.

Louis Levauchelle had joined us in November 1915. His wound was very similar to mine and to those of several other wounded men on our floor. A hole in the middle of the face, as if the flesh had been sucked in from the inside. He had already undergone three attempted grafts, in hospitals with less of a reputation than ours, first with the cartilage of a pig, then a sow, then a calf. All three rejected.

71

He kept photographs of his wife and two sons by his bedside, photographs that had stayed with him through all the fourteen months of fighting.

Levauchelle often made up a fourth at *belote*.

During the early months of the war, the military hierarchy had encouraged men with maxillofacial wounds to stay in their hospitals, even when their condition allowed them to go out. The open display of our wounds might have been a blow to the morale of a nation waging a war which was no closer to an end and which demanded a growing commitment. Visits were authorized sparingly and took place in a room on the ground floor that resembled a classroom in a Parisian secondary school on examination day, with two desks and four chairs.

Levauchelle wrote often to his family, but like the rest of us, he had never had the courage to admit how serious his condition was.

His first visit from his wife and children took place on 21 June 1916, the first day of summer.

That morning, Levauchelle asked our advice as to what day clothes would be the most appropriate. He hesitated between keeping his bandages on, wearing a black headband, and simply leaving his wounds exposed. I recommended the headband, thinking that it would be the least upsetting. He was as agitated as a child.

I can still see his tall figure coming back along the corridor to the ward after the visit. When he saw me, he collapsed on my shoulder, in no state even to speak. He dropped onto his bed, and Weil and I stood by him, powerless to do anything, until night fell. When the lights were turned out, we left him.

The next morning, knowing from experience that the moment of waking was the most difficult time to get through, I got up and approached his bed. If I had not lost my sense of smell, the odour of spilled blood would have alerted me. He had taken his own life.

The day before, he had asked a nurse to buy him a packet of sweets for his children. As she felt he might be unsteady on his feet, she had suggested she accompany him to the visiting room.

Neither his wife nor his children had recognized him. The elder of the two boys had run off down the corridor, screaming: 'Not my daddy! Not my daddy!' His wife had taken the children by the hand, promising to come back when he was more 'himself'.

A mass was said for Louis in the hospital chapel. Four of his ward companions, those whose sense of balance had not been affected by their wounds, took part. The priest officiated in a monotonous voice – he must have been performing one funeral service after another for many months on end.

I learned from Penanster that it had taken him a long time to persuade the priest to say mass for a suicide. In the middle of the service, Marguerite appeared, a tall figure with her face concealed behind a scarf, and knelt in the back row.

At the end of the service, we all came out together. Penanster, who was in front, stopped in the corridor that led back to the wards, turned and made us swear with him that none of us would take his own life. The body was taken away to be buried in a place called Marnes-la-Coquette. Sometimes, the name of a place is quite inappropriate to the circumstances.

Weil suggested that we should ask for permission to go out on 14 July. I was not keen on the idea, but Penanster agreed that it was time to confront the world. For Marguerite, it was still much too early.

We debated for a while what to wear, and finally decided to go out in uniform and head bandages. I had managed to retrieve my own uniform. By some miracle, it had reached the hospital laundry, and when it was returned to me it was spotless – I had expected to find it as disfigured as I was. Penanster borrowed a uniform from a cavalry officer on the first floor. Weil could not lay his hands on an aviator's uniform, and finally squeezed into that of an infantry lieutenant. The sleeves of his tunic only reached as far as mid-arm, and his trousers barely covered his socks.

Our 'lost squadron' set off about eleven in the morning. I don't recall ever in my life having known such intense fear. Even before the most major operations, I had never felt such anguish, or been so dizzy. It was as if I had been asked to cross Paris jumping from one roof to another.

We headed towards the Seine, Penanster in front, head held high, easily the most presentable of the three of us. Then came Weil, looking straight ahead. I brought up the rear, my eyes on the ground, staring intently at the manhole covers.

The sky was a faded blue, with high clouds scurrying in the wind.

An old man coming home from his morning constitutional stopped on the doorstep of his building, looked us slowly up and down, one after the other, and raised his hat to salute us.

The fresh air bothered me – I had never before realized there could be so much of it. Like anything of which there is a surfeit, it soon became oppressive.

Paris seemed deserted. There were just a few women and old people about. It was as if the whole country had emigrated.

Fifty metres away, and heading straight for us, was a whole herd of children led by a young blonde woman. It was time to turn back. I tugged at my friends' sleeves. But Weil was determined to buy himself a croissant. We tried our best to explain to him that bread was already becoming scarce, but he was adamant. It was as if he wanted to give our excursion a purpose. We spotted a bakery on the corner of the boulevard. The window was empty. There was a woman inside, polishing the display shelf, with her back to us. Weil entered the shop first, with us hard on his heels, like carriages attached to a locomotive. The woman turned. Her eyes opened wide, and she dropped her cloth and a loaf of black bread she had been holding in her other hand. The loaf rolled along the floor and stopped at Weil's feet. Without giving him time to pick it up, the woman rushed to seize her merchandise, as if snatching her child from the hands of a stranger. The loaf nestling in her arms, she retreated behind the counter. Pretending to ignore her terror, Penanster stepped forward.

'Three croissants, please,' he asked her, very politely.

'Croissants?' she replied. 'Croissants? You must be joking! All I have is two loaves of black bread, and they're already sold.' She stared at us with an air of finality. 'You're not Germans, by any chance?'

Weil burst into loud laughter, and we turned on our heels and left. My whole body was shaking, as if it were suddenly the middle of winter. I begged my friends to go back, and Penanster and Weil concurred.

When, some time later, I suggested they go out again without me, they proposed a game of cards instead, making the excuse that I had fleeced them the day before.

We never again mentioned that disastrous outing.

Whenever we talked about the past, we rarely went back further than our mobilization.

Weil often spoke of how exhilarating it had been to fly over the German lines. He said he sometimes couldn't stop his limbs trembling when he got into the cockpit after an enemy plane had been spotted, but the fear disappeared as soon as the propeller began to turn. Once he was in the air, he felt invincible, as if life had become unreal. Even today, he had only one thought in his head – to fly again.

Just as I liked to make him talk about this experience

whom he was proud to number himself, and the merely superstitious. 'The first give,' he would say. 'The second give in order to receive.' He thought that man, in his quest for certainty, was on the road to ruin, that God had given man a degree of consciousness that allowed him to understand the great questions, but that He had never intended him to answer them – that was a task He had reserved for Himself. Penanster called it the great misunderstanding. To him, religion meant something quite different from the caricatured teachings of my childhood, or the believers I had known, whose faith was nothing but a will to dominate through morality.

But for me, it was too late.

When my own father had felt his last hour approaching, five years before, he had summoned us, my sister and me, so that we could drink a toast to his departure. I went down into the cellar hurriedly to find a bottle of champagne, knowing full well that the first drops would finish him off. As he raised the glass to his lips, I knew that he was preparing to never see us again, here or elsewhere. Up until the very last moment, I thought he was going to send for a priest, he whose mother went to mass twice a day. Not a bit of it. He expired without the least thought for eternal life. He had proclaimed the end of his existence to his children, and had not left them the slightest hope that we would ever meet again.

Not to believe was for him the highest form of courage, and he had given us a perfect example of it. In the process, he had turned me away from religion forever.

★

We never talked about the future, but I was gradually starting to think about it more and more. It seemed likely to be as painful as the past. Perhaps more so. The past had taken us by surprise, like lightning hitting a tree, whereas the future was creeping up on us like an old man. The immediate future seemed the most terrifying. One of these days, we would have to make up our minds to leave for good. I think Penanster and Weil were relieved when I had given up after our first attempt, but we knew we would have to try again. We had a good excuse for postponing the day – the newcomers who were arriving by the trainload from Verdun. The capacity of the maxillofacial service had been doubled. There was plenty to keep us busy. Every week, one of the newcomers tried to kill himself by slitting his wrists or hanging himself from the cistern in the toilets. The veterans among us had to persuade youngsters who had lost one or more of their senses that there were still valid reasons to live. But it would not take them long to realize that not only had they lost taste, smell, hearing or sight, but they also had to bid a fond farewell to sexual desire.

The newcomers, tempted as they were by self-pity, were impressed by Penanster, whose courage was clear in his every gesture and every word, and startled by Weil, whose jokes made everyone laugh – even those who no longer had a mouth. He told them that he was planning to sue the doctors because of the temporary nose they had given him, a painted aluminium nose as straight as a nun's.

The story his audience enjoyed the most was the one

about a lieutenant-colonel, a senator's son, slightly wounded in the cheek, who had demanded a private room – which of course had been refused him.

Everyone wondered what he was doing in the hospital – his wound was scarcely as big as a scratch from a thorn. It was clear he missed women a lot. He had noticed that at the top of the partition wall in the toilets, there was a hole as wide as a bull's eye through which you could see the nurse's latrines. One day, he climbed up on the toilet bowl, stood on tiptoe, and let out an agonizing scream. The lieutenant-colonel had slipped to the bottom of the bowl, and got his foot caught in the hole, breaking a bone in the process.

Weil moved from one man to another like a cat, trying to spot the most vulnerable. He organized card contests. He taught chess. He had even reconstructed, in a corner of the ward, a sort of plane cabin, where he taught the rudiments of flying to newcomers languishing between operations. And none of the patients was allowed to leave without a model biplane made out of cardboard or wood.

Something strange happened one day, something that brought my future into sharper focus for a while. One morning, as I was doing my usual circuit of the floor to stretch my legs, I heard an unexpected commotion from the stairwell. A big black man, a Senegalese, as naked as a worm, was being chased by two nurses and a surgeon all tangled up in his gown. He had woken up during his operation, as soon as the knife went in, and had run away as fast as he could. He got as far as the guard post before they caught up with him.

I immediately had the idea of going to Africa once the war was over. It was said that the natives respected men with severe wounds.

An artillery lieutenant told me how his uncle, disfigured in '70, had re-enlisted in the colonial service to give himself a greater field of opportunity. He had told him that in Africa a disfigured warrior was treated like a lord.

I mentioned my idea to Weil, whose first thought was of the women.

'I doubt they distinguish much between a handsome white man and a disfigured one. What's more, it's said they have remarkable bodies – even if their bottoms are a bit on the large side. I like this African idea of yours! I propose a partnership. We'll take two or three planes. I'll take care of the flying, you can handle the mechanical side. We'll be a sensation.'

For a time, this prospect gave us a new sense of determination, like any dream you want to believe in even if you know it'll never come true.

Penanster was sitting on the little bench in the convalescents' yard. The sun, falling on his good profile, the one he had conserved almost whole, gave a glint to his green eye as he looked at us out of the corner of it. It was a summer's day in 1916. I remember it well because I had the biggest surprise of my life that day.

Penanster was puffing peacefully on his English cigarette.

He began to talk in that grave voice of his, a voice that

still retained all its splendour, even though his broken teeth gave it a slightly sibilant edge.

'My friends,' he began – he seemed solemn and embarrassed at the same time – 'we cannot neglect our senses.'

Weil threw me a sidelong glance.

'I suggest an excursion. We have to confront the eyes of women. Afterwards, it will be too late – the lack of confidence will have got the better of us. This is the moment to take action.

'I know,' he went on, as if anticipating our reaction, 'that, coming from me, this must seem shocking to you, but this is one area where we need to depart from the normal moral framework. In this situation, we cannot be bound by the trivial anxieties of the well-to-do bourgeois.'

He paused for a moment.

'Our first outing was not what we might call a success. We abdicated collectively.' He pointed at Weil. 'The two of us as much as Adrien, isn't that so?'

Weil acquiesced without a word.

'My friends,' Penanster concluded, 'I am therefore taking the liberty of suggesting a trip to the nearest brothel. This is a sacred duty, are we all agreed?'

I expected him to unfold a military map and draw a circle round the target. And since our friend had just explained that we were under orders, it was with a light heart that we agreed to fight this battle.

We obtained permission to go out two days later in the

afternoon. Our second outing in two years – it was not as if we were taking undue advantage.

The mixture of mission and schoolboys' escapade was not unpleasing to me. I sensed that Weil did not feel quite the same way, although of the three of us he was the one who had most of an eye for the ladies. On reflection, it was probably for that very reason that he was the least at ease.

Penanster left our hospital fortress at the head of the procession. He was not wearing any bandages. Weil followed, all his wounds exposed, his great toffee face, as he himself described it, displayed to the world. As for me, I had covered my wounds with my black head bandage, which hid the worst.

The brothel was a few minutes' walk from the Val-de-Grâce, in a little street near Montparnasse, at the end of a courtyard surrounded by artists' studios.

We stood for a few minutes observing the front door of the establishment. Two respectable-looking men came out.

The whole thing was just like a military operation. We waited until the coast was clear, then Penanster approached the door. Before knocking, he stopped and turned to us.

'There is nothing more pitiless than the eyes of a prostitute, is there?' he said in a low voice, as if to convince himself.

Weil replied that as none of us had a mother-in-law, it was hard to say for certain.

The madam who opened the door was exactly what

we might have expected. She had a face like a fish, grotesquely made-up as if for a carnival, and her skin was so slack that its folds looked like tiers of balconies.

The place was of modest proportions and blatant bad taste. The purple colour of the walls gave the room a false air of opulence, and the Second Empire furniture was straight out of a country attic.

There were two old gentlemen sitting comfortably, reading newspapers, their faces shrouded in cigar smoke. They appeared to be waiting their turn.

When the madam clapped eyes on the three of us, she made no attempt to conceal her surprise.

'Well, well, my poor boys, they really messed you up, didn't they? I'm sorry, I don't have any girls available at the moment. In any case, I'm not sure they'd accept.'

'They probably prefer old men, or shirkers!' Penanster retorted. 'Or perhaps men who pulled strings to get themselves declared unfit. Maybe even Boches!'

'I'll see what I can do,' the woman said, grinning like a turkey and revealing a row of decaying teeth. 'Sit yourselves down in the corner and have a drink. But please stay there. I wouldn't like our other clients to . . . You understand. Well, anyway, I'll be back in a moment. I hope at least you have money?'

From the look Penanster gave her, she realized the question was misplaced. She returned ten minutes later, pulling by the hand two dishevelled young women who were trying to straighten their dresses.

'These three gentlemen have come specially for you, ladies. I want you to make our house proud of you.'

I encouraged Penanster and Weil to go first. The madam assured me that I would not have much longer to wait, and withdrew, waddling like a duck.

A door hidden behind a curtain opened and an elegant young man came out. He did not seem at all bothered at being seen. A moment later, a girl approached me. I doubted she was even twenty. Her blonde hair was tousled, and her florid cheeks were the only touch of colour in an otherwise pale face.

She said hello like a little girl being introduced to some distant great-uncle.

I closed the door behind me.

She stripped off boldly and without the least trace of provocation. Then she stood there in the middle of the room, waiting for me to tell her what I wanted.

Her body was perfect, which added to my embarrassment.

'I must say, mademoiselle, I think you are very beautiful, and to be frank, absolutely to my taste. Nobody forced me to come here, not at all. It was more a kind of wager that I made with my friends.'

She was clearly bored by my speech, but at the same time grateful that I was giving her a brief respite.

'To tell the truth,' I went on, 'I've never set foot in a place like this before, and never would have, if it hadn't been for that stupid wager . . . So as we have a little time, perhaps we could talk?'

'Old men who can't do it any more always ask if we can talk. Are you old, too?'

I made no reply.

'Did you get that in the war?'

'Yes.'

'You're lucky. My brother was killed.'

'Yes, I've certainly been lucky.'

'Well, what shall we do? Talk or do something? With that bandage over your mouth, it's hard to understand what you're saying.'

Without dressing again, she sat down on the corner of the bed, her knees together.

The desire I felt and my sense of dignity were doing battle inside me.

As I stared at her, the images of two other women's faces were superimposed on hers. The faces of Clémence and Marguerite. Love and respect.

Desire overcame both.

Afterwards, I had to confront the sadness that takes hold of you when the act has been consummated without love.

Getting dressed again, and to assuage my conscience, I tried to be as kind to her as I could. I would only have made myself look ridiculous if I had suggested taking her away from there. I still had enough sense of propriety not to do that. I promised I would come and see her again soon, which was the least of her worries.

Penanster and Weil were waiting for me in the little boudoir near the entrance. From the way they looked at me, I sensed that I had been rather a long time.

We paid without haggling, and even left a generous tip.

On the way back, Penanster offered us each without a

word one of those English cigarettes he had somehow obtained, and which tasted of travel.

We did not exchange a single word all the way, each of us lost in his own thoughts.

It was Weil who broke the silence as we were approaching the guard post:

'It's always the same, when you're having a bad time. You think you've been through the worst, you think you've endured all a man can endure. But you're wrong – there's always something else. All we needed was syphilis. We've probably got that now, as well.'

We never again mentioned the episode among ourselves, judging there was nothing else to be said. The most difficult thing was evading Marguerite's questions, discreet as they were, about our escapade.

The summer of 1916 passed like the previous one. I had the advantage of only being operated on once. Penanster underwent a new attempt at a bone graft, which failed.

Weil received two skin grafts.

But the advantage was still mine. We each kept count of our operations by making notches in a piece of wood, and I still had a respectable lead.

My score was seven. Penanster and Weil were equal with five each.

Every day, the war brought us an increasing number of men with mutilated faces. The respiratory complications caused by poison gas made the surgeons' task more difficult. But we were satisfied with our work. Not a single suicide attempt since June.

Our relationship to time changed. The idea of the future faded. We lived in the present, if not in the moment. And in pain, a constant if uninvited guest who tried to fool us by pretending he was leaving for good, only to return with a violence that never failed to surprise us. The days were endless, with nothing in store. The war was taking place far away, behind a curtain of smoke. The young ones remained alert to any news from the front, any sign of a major advance. The old ones, believing our cause was just, never doubted we would win in the end, but kept aloof from the excessive enthusiasm that greeted every new development. We ended up dreading these fleeting escapes from lethargy. Whenever this war of shifting positions moved even a little, there were so many deaths that no man in the ward was immune from bad news about a father, a brother, a friend cut down amid the hordes of dead. It all added to the misery of our situation.

The letters I exchanged with my family were still so banal they allowed me to stick to the everyday, avoiding giving the least information about my wounds. I had nothing to say to them for fear of divulging the reality of my condition, and I was not very good at inventing. But I continued to send one letter a week, endlessly repeating the details of my menus − chopped meat, soup − and asking as many qestions as I could about the health of the people I had known. Whenever they informed me that one of my friends from the village or from school had had an arm or a leg amputated, I felt relieved, saying to myself: 'At least there's one who's out of it!'

Every time I wrote, memories of home would come flooding back. I remembered those autumn mornings when I would set off for the forest with my father and grandfather. It was my grandfather who would launch the plan of battle the previous evening, with learned calculations that combined the phases of the moon, the duration of the latest rains and the intensity of the sunshine that had followed. We were usually given the verdict at the end of supper, when my mother rose to clear the table. My grandfather would sit there deep in thought, his chin resting on the flat of his fists. The ritual was always the same.

As long as nobody asked him anything, he would say nothing. Then the question would come.

'Hey, Grandad, will there be any?'

He would sit for another minute or two in silence, not moving, not giving the least hint of what his reply would be.

At last he would deliver his verdict.

'There might be a few . . .'

I would start to jump up and down on my chair like a young goat. We still had to know the likely size of the harvest, to be prepared.

'Shall we take the baskets or the potato sacks, Granddad?'

If he replied the sacks, that meant we would get more than ten kilos of wild mushrooms the next day. In the autumn of 1913, in the first two weeks of October, the daily tally was as many as forty kilos. Half went to the family and the rest went into jars.

Nobody knew every little nook and cranny like my grandfather. When we entered the forest early in the morning, he would stop and take a deep breath.

'There you are, my boy, smell the earth steaming!'

A subtle but persistent mixture of damp earth, bracken and chestnut leaves would delight my senses.

I would never smell that scent again. And whenever I thought of it, I was moved to tears. I found my deformity easier to accept than my incurable loss of taste and smell.

The winter of 1916 was one winter too many.

Bonnard had sent me a jubilant letter in the middle of October, telling me he had finally managed to get sent to the front. He was being assigned to the artillery. I assumed they were going to use him to calculate trajectories, not to actually fire the guns.

On 23 December, I received a letter from his mother, telling me that Alain had been killed in a bombardment. Until then, I had never had any doubts about the war or the need to wage it. I had been prepared to suffer, even to die. Now it had taken my oldest friend from me, the one who, in my mind, should have been the last to perish. I felt totally helpless. I hadn't been there to protect him, to cover his body with mine when the shell had fallen. Curiously, I had the feeling of being face to face with death for the first time. I had known other men who had died, often people who had been close to me, but Bonnard and I had shared one mind. It was what I imagined losing a twin brother must feel like.

The war was becoming absurd, and the very fact that

we recognized it as such made us vulnerable. How far would we have to go before there was any sign of an end to it? Even our little village in the Dordogne already boasted three men dead and one disfigured. And we had not advanced a single inch.

I had been counting on Alain for afterwards. I needed his friendship to return to civilian life, to help me to accept the looks other people would give me, but it was clear now that this war had no respect for anything – it had taken Bonnard.

On the morning of 2 February 1917, the ward sister entered and came straight up to me, a triumphant smile on her lips.

'Lieutenant Fournier, you have a visitor! I told her you were here and in top form. She's waiting for you in the visiting room.'

'Who is it?'

I felt as if an ambush was being prepared for me.

'Your sister. She presented herself at the guard post.'

'My sister? Good Lord!'

'You don't seem pleased.'

'On the contrary, I'm delighted.' I paused. 'Delighted. But can't you tell her I'm not feeling well? She could come back in a few days.'

'But Lieutenant, I just told her you were on top form! She seemed so worried, the poor girl. She even asked me if you had lost an arm or a leg. I told her not a bit of it, you were intact.'

'Intact? That was the word you used – intact?'

'Of course, Lieutenant.'

The woman had seen too much. She no longer realized.

'Hurry up! She's waiting for you, and she's so excited!'

I felt like vomiting. I trembled as I dressed. Penanster lent me his biggest head bandage. I remembered Levauchelle. I swore to myself that whatever happened I would keep my dignity and not let myself be upset.

I saw her from the end of the corridor. She looked quite small. She was pacing up and down, biting her nails furiously. She had put on a beautiful dress, just for me. I wanted so much to protect her, but it was too late, I could not retreat. I suppose it was the hesitant way I was walking along the corridor, with light flooding in from the convalescents' yard, which first caught her eye. She came towards me, walking like the well-brought-up girl she was.

Then I saw her lift her hands to her eyes, before she came up to me and collapsed against my chest. I did not move.

We sat down side by side in the visiting room. She placed her head on my shoulder and we stayed like that for a while, as silent as two lovers waiting for a train that will take one of them away.

I talked on and on, about her, an adolescent when I had left, a woman now. I recalled the arguments we'd had as children, the fights.

Before she left, I told her to take care of our family. At least she had recognized me, I said – not all my comrades had been so lucky.

She went away, unsteady on her feet, promising to return soon.

I wondered if she would have the strength.

A few weeks later, my mother was announced.

As was her habit, she could not keep still, and had to pry in every corner. She showered me with unimportant news, drew up an exhaustive catalogue of my wounds, and made various arrangements, all relating to material things. Anything material reinforced her optimism.

There was something both exasperating and reassuring about my mother. She was incapable of seeing the tragic side of things.

Her son had not been disfigured. At the very most, he had been deprived of certain parts of his organism, which were therefore clearly not indispensable.

My mother's limited intelligence had survived the shadow of my father's personality. Now that he was gone, she had reverted to her true nature – that of a squirrel hoarding food for the winter.

The year 1917 went by without any notable event. The three of us were perfectly equal that year. Two operations each.

The days dragged by, idly, in a kind of emotional numbness. The major offensive launched by General Nivelle jolted us out of this paralysis. The carnage that resulted was so great that for the first time, men with severe facial injuries had to be accommodated in the corridors. For the first time, too, we were aware of stirrings of rebellion among the troops who had been sent to the front needlessly. Even the officers had lost their pride in doing a job that had to be done. Those who were still capable made no bones about what they thought of the idiots on the general staff.

The entry of the Americans into the war reassured us. Maybe it was all going to end.

The smell of ether made me sick, even from the far end of a corridor. It was the only smell that managed to reach me.

The surgeon was still trying to give me a mouth that functioned normally, but the results did not live up to his claims and made no significant change in my everyday life.

Marguerite was given extended leave towards the end of summer 1918. The surgeon had managed to strengthen the outer shell of her face, which had been less damaged than ours, even though her appearance was just as seriously affected. He thought it a good idea to give her a respite of several weeks before proceeding with what he called 'the finishing touches'. We had a lot of respect for our doctors, and they themselves treated us with consideration, but the results of these 'finishing touches' of theirs did not live up to their expectations, despite all the advances that had been made since the beginning of the war.

Marguerite came to see us twice a week and we spent more time with her than we had when she'd been in the hospital and the nurses had tended to erect a barrier between her and the men.

Penanster called our friend's extended leave a punishment. It was as if our little world was the only one where we all felt safe.

Marguerite had returned home without letting anyone know in advance. She had rung at the service entrance. The maid, who did not know her, had taken her for a pedlar and slammed the door in her face. She next rang at the front door. An old manservant opened. Her parents were giving a reception that evening. The old man, who had been in her family's service for more than forty years, recoiled, then lifted his hand to his mouth. She could lip-read well enough to make out his words.

'Mademoiselle Marguerite, I don't know what to say . . . We weren't expecting you . . . I'll tell Madame and Monsieur.'

Her parents appeared in evening dress, They showed no warmth towards her, but that was no surprise. After all, she thought, why change the habits of a lifetime? Nor was she surprised by their embarrassment. It was hard not to feel ill at ease when confronted with wounds like those, especially on a woman. But the main reason for their embarrassment was that Marguerite was disturbing their party. The staff were assembled and ordered to look after her and give her whatever she wanted. In return, she had to agree to stay in her room. Her brothers put in a brief appearance a little later in the evening, both drunk and both offhand. The two of them had been declared unfit. One suffered from tuberculosis, which was indeed something to weigh against a war, and their father had pulled strings to get the other exempted, too – the likely loss of one son was misfortune enough. Neither enquired about their sister's condition.

'You'll see, Marguerite,' they told her, casually. 'Doctors can perform miracles nowadays. Actually,' they added, 'you could have given us a bit more news. We were worried stiff. We'll see you tomorrow. Let's enjoy this little party while we can. Wartime is so boring.'

That very same evening, Marguerite took the decision to leave her touching little family forever. She did so during the night. She was fairly pleased with herself and her level of lip-reading. She reflected that her parents liked the sound of their own voices as much as ever – they had not even noticed that she was deaf.

She went to a little hotel in the rue St Honoré, and from there went in search of a room, which she found the very next day. While waiting for further grafts, she began work again as a nurse in the Hospital for Sick Children.

Between one wave of casualties and the next, the war was again imposing its rhythm on us. Each frantic influx of disfigured patients was followed by a short period of calm. But this time, we were sure, the number of casualties indicated that victory was near.

I was the doyen of the floor, the one who had spent the whole of the war in the hospital. I had become a sort of oracle to the newcomers. As soon as they regained consciousness, they would come to ask me questions about what would happen next.

Under the impetus of the old timers, our community

of men with facial wounds was beginning to organize, and to express itself.

Some wrote poems in honour of faceless men, while others produced a newspaper entitled *The General Graft*. How regularly it appeared depended on the surgery its editors had to undergo.

The news of the armistice, on 11 November, unleashed a great wave of joy on our floor. We all embraced, some shaken by unstoppable sobs. It was also a huge relief – it had not all been for nothing. Absorbed as we were in the joy of victory, we did not notice that the young man from Marseilles who had been brought in two days earlier, and whose teeth had not stopped chattering since, had died quietly in his corner. That was our last death.

B Y the twelfth of November, the jubilation we had all felt at the victory had subsided again, like autumn leaves fallen from the trees.

We thought of what demobilization must be like, all those men returning to their families safe and sound. As long as they had been out there at the front, in the mud and the cold, waiting for the next offensive, we had been able to consider ourselves lucky – they were risking more than us.

Now that the guns had fallen silent, and legions of demobilized soldiers were being reunited happily with their nearest and dearest, we felt like the lowest of mortals.

In the five months between the armistice and my coming out of hospital, I underwent two further operations, to 'draw a veil', as they put it, over the chasm that was forever mine.

I left the Val de Grâce on the morning of 4 April 1919. An icy rain was falling. Despite sixteen operations, my face still did not look human, but at least I had the most impressive collection of pirate headbands to hide my wounds.

Penanster and Weil were due to follow a few weeks

later. We said goodbye, promising to see each other again as soon as possible, and for the first time I saw a tear in the corner of the Breton's eye.

Weil concealed his emotion with a final boast.

'Just think of all the women who've been waiting for us on the other side of those railings for the last five years!'

Time can be a great deceiver. I had expected to find Paris still caught up in the joy of victory. I had imagined that the party would still be going on when I returned and that I would walk down the boulevard Saint Michel on a mattress of confetti and streamers. Instead of that, the monster seemed asleep.

It was the women who had kept it at bay, and they seemed worn out from the effort of carrying the burden alone. In this city where things were getting back to normal, the men who were young and whole seemed few and far between and were viewed almost with suspicion because they had not got themselves killed. One might have imagined that after a war as total as this one, there would be great changes. Nothing of the sort – everyone went back to their habits, as if putting on a pair of old slippers. This return to normality reminded me of an event I had lived through a few years before. In the autumn of 1912, the stables of the château of Peyrelevade had caught fire, in the section where the fodder was stored. Like all the young men in the area, I rushed to help. Among the horses I rescued was a big saddle horse, his eyes bulging with uncontrollable terror, who almost tore my arm off as I held his halter. One minute, the beast was shaking with panic and foaming at the mouth. The next, he was peacefully grazing on the edge of a clump of flowers.

It is difficult to talk of convalescence after four years and eight months in a white prison.

I didn't yet feel quite brave enough to go back to my little apartment, where the memory of Clémence still hovered. I therefore accepted an offer from my uncle Chaumontel to come and recharge my batteries, as he put it.

He was my mother's eldest brother. He had married, late in life, a woman much younger than himself, who had borne him three daughters before dying of tuberculosis in 1911.

The three girls, who were barely out of their teens, fêted me as a hero. I loved their freshness and their kindness towards me. Their warmth quite turned my head after five years in an exclusively male world.

Still weak from my last operation, I would sit in a wicker chaise longue under the pride of the grounds, a big cedar of Lebanon, and stare in wonder like a child at all the comings and goings of a house that bustled with life.

There never seemed to be an end to the activity. The staff would constantly be busy putting up tables and arranging bouquets of flowers. My uncle liked the house to be full, and I rediscovered those long Sunday lunches that begin at midday and drift on until five in the afternoon, with all the guests scattered about the grounds in the shade of the trees. True, the food wasn't quite what we had known before the war, but the bottles of Burgundy had improved with age. Not that I could taste it, but I liked the illusory sense of well-being that drunkenness brought.

My mother and sisters joined us for two weeks. My eldest cousin's suitor also spent some time with us. There were seventeen rooms in this paradise on the banks of the Marne, at Nogent, and they were never empty.

I had written to my employers, Nallet and Grichard, to inform them that I wished to start work again at the beginning of July, which seemed to give me enough time for my convalescence. I had not gone into too much detail about the nature of my wounds.

Monsieur Grichard replied by letter that he would see me before then, to work out the details of our future collaboration. We agreed to meet in May.

I took a train to the Gare de Lyon and from there a tram to the rue de Milan.

I had forgotten how hot and crowded Parisian transport could be, and my first reflex was to flee people's glances, in which I saw a mixture of pity, compassion and embarrassment.

The war had been over for six months, but its remnants would still be walking around for many years to come. The looks my fellow citizens gave me made it clear they would take a long time to accept us.

Some men, most often middle-aged, showed their gratitude by raising their hats as I passed. In the tram and in the metro, passengers stood to leave me the place reserved for war invalids. But I declined the offer.

'Thank you,' I said. 'My legs are fine.'

Naturally, the concierge at 9 rue de Milan did not recognize me.

'And you are—?'

'Adrien Fournier, Madame Robillard.'

'The young engineer who started here in March 1914?'

'That's right.'

'Oh, my God, I'm really sorry . . .'

'There's no need, Madame Robillard, no need.'

I was going to have to get used to hearing these condolences for the survivor.

'Are you expected?'

'Yes, by Monsieur Grichard.'

Old Grichard was a short man who tried to appear taller than he was by adopting a military bearing. He was the co-founder of Nallet and Grichard. I had never liked him much, thinking him as honest as a snake.

He shook my hand, avoiding my eyes, and offered me a seat. Then he lit a cigarette, and let his eyes wander towards the window.

'Monsieur Fournier,' he said, 'you mentioned in your letter than you had been wounded, but I had no idea your wounds were so severe. Chemin des Dames, Verdun, the Somme?'

'An ambush in the Meuse, in 'fourteen.'

'I beg your pardon? I didn't quite catch that.'

'I said an ambush in the Meuse, in 'fourteen.'

My diction was still far from perfect, but I thought I had made myself clear.

'An ambush in the Meuse in 'fourteen and you've only just come out of hospital? Those damned Bosches certainly didn't do things by halves! Was it a deep wound?'

'Somewhat . . .'

'I beg your pardon?'

The letter *s* was still fairly difficult for me to pronounce, demanding an agility of the palate that was no longer mine to command.

'I said: Somewhat deep . . .'

I would have happily stuck my tongue out at him through my nose, but I did not dare.

'Ah, yes, I see. And in your opinion, how many months will it take before you've recovered?'

'I *have* recovered, sir.'

'You *have* recovered? Forgive me. I was only asking, of course. And you wish to start work with us again?'

'That's right, sir. I'd like to get back to my old job.'

He tugged thoughtfully at his beard.

'Difficult, difficult . . .' he continued, in such a low voice that I had the impression he would rather not be speaking at all.

'I beg your pardon?'

'I said: Difficult. I shan't beat about the bush. Our situation here is not very good. We used to build bridges and tunnels, and of course during a war nobody wants such things. Today, with all the damage caused by the war, there are new possibilities but the question is: Who's going to pay? The State's coffers are empty. The Boches haven't yet paid a penny. It's a serious problem.

'And there is another one, Monsieur Fournier. Please don't take this personally, but in your state, I can no longer employ you as a commercial engineer. You appreciate the difficulty. Nothing personal, Fournier, nothing personal. I don't need a technical engineer. Plassard, who was declared unfit for service in 'fourteen because of his weak lungs, is managing very well. He's completely mastered his field. We're very satisfied with him. He's made a lot of progress in these last five years.

'As you can see, your situation poses real problems. Think about it, and if you don't find a solution by yourself, we'll try to make an effort. There may be something for you in the research department, if you can't find anything else. Not as an engineer, unfortunately, but something comfortable, without too many outside contacts. But please think about it. Do the rounds, and if you like, we can talk again. In any case, you can rest assured we shan't leave a war hero in the lurch.'

'Monsieur Grichard,' I said, 'I'd like to insist on the fact that I was wounded in the war – wounded, not crippled.'

'Oh, absolutely. I'm perfectly well aware of the difference. Let's leave it at that for the moment, if you don't mind. I'll see you to the door. Keep in touch and we'll sort something out. So long, Monsieur Fournier.'

I took the seven o'clock train, as if I were returning from a day's work. On the way, I again thought of Africa as the promised land. I imagined those big black men bowing low as the warlord passed. I'd have to talk to Weil again about our project. And those looks . . . When would they all stop looking at me?

The whole family were at table under the big cedar. As I arrived, they all stood up at the same time and began to clap, with tears in their eyes. My eldest cousin, Adèle, threw her arms around my neck. My sister Pauline took me by the hand, wiping her eyes with a sleeve.

My uncle approached, a glass in his hand, taking his time, savouring the news he was about to impart.

'Nephew, you have a letter from Clémenceau.' He seemed pleased with the effect of his words. 'A letter from the Tiger himself!'

I wondered what the Prime Minister could possibly write to an officer they were getting ready to reinstate in a research office, a cubby hole under the stairs that received natural light three hours a day.

I took the letter and read it aloud. Everyone held their breath.

The heading was indeed that of the Prime Minister, and the style was indeed that of someone in a position of great power. Firstly, I was informed that I was to be made a Chevalier of the Legion of Honour. Secondly, that I had been chosen to be one of a delegation of seriously wounded Frenchmen who would be presented to the heads of state who were to sign the treaty of Versailles.

I knew it was a moment that would always loom large in my memory, and I felt enormous pride. In an instant, I had moved from the research department to the peace treaty ending a world war. This small contribution to the history of my country was like the long-awaited acknowledgement of our sacrifice.

The event was celebrated late into the night, like a success in the school exams. The whole family gathered around me, pampering me like the prodigal son. Their warmth brought me solace – something I was only just beginning to admit that I needed. I feared that my mother would spoil this wonderful evening with one of those stupid remarks that only she could make, but it did not happen.

The next day I asked my cousin to accompany me to my apartment, where I wanted to pick up some of my civilian things. Her somewhat roguish good looks gave me a sense of security as we crossed Paris. I used her as a bait to divert people's looks from me. She played the game well, entering into the spirit of it to such an extent that those who saw her pressing herself against me in the tram must have wondered about the true nature of our relationship.

Nobody had entered the apartment since that August night in 1914 when my encounter with Clémence had led me to postpone my departure.

The entrance was as dark as ever. The concierge had her back to us. Lifting Adèle in my arms, I hurried in. She clung to my shoulder. The effort made me feel dizzy. My body never tired of reminding me how much it had been neglected during the years at Val de Grâce. Telling

Adèle that the apartment was bound to be extremely dirty and untidy after being empty for five years, I asked her to let me go in alone.

I headed straight for the bedroom, without a glance at the other rooms. The window was still half-open, the lace curtain blowing in the breeze. The bed was still unmade. I tried to find a shape in the arrangement of the sheets that would show me she had returned, that she had stayed in this room during my absence. I peered into the smallest nook in search of a letter, a note, a scrap of paper with a few hastily scribbled words, anything.

She had not even pulled up the blankets. She must have left hurriedly at dawn, riddled with guilt.

I sat down on the edge of the bed and began to cry. Adèle tiptoed into the room, as if I were asleep and she were afraid to wake me. She placed her hands on my head, studiously avoiding looking at my tear-stained face. We left again for Nogent.

On the way back, Adèle tried everything she could to rouse me from my numbness. She told me about her suitor, and how unsure she was of his feelings. I realized that I had become a sort of confidant to her. The fact that I had difficulty in speaking made me a good listener.

She asked me questions about love, about the everyday life of a couple, and other things I could not answer. It was an unusual kind of conversation for a young girl and an older man to have. But to her, the fact that I was thirty years old meant that I was a man of the world, even if I had been out of it for five years.

I was more overjoyed to be reunited with Penanster and Weil than to be taking part in a historic event. I recognized two other friends from Val de Grâce whom I had met several times in the privates' ward. A military car had come to pick us up at the Invalides to drive us to Versailles, where the peace treaty was to be signed.

An aide-de-camp led us through a crowd of gentlemen in hats, civilian and military, speaking different languages. These men from all nations, most of them old, had gathered there in that palace to decide the future of war and peace, their motives surely very different from the motives of those who had pushed us into fighting. What impressed me most was not that I was in the company of statesmen like Clémenceau, but that I was seeing Germans for real – and for the first time.

It struck me that it must be a terrible thing not just to be wounded, as we were, but defeated too, like the Germans. Not that there was any compassion in the thought. I felt a stream of bile filling me as the German delegation entered the Hall of Mirrors, their stiff dignity clearly intended to counterbalance the weight of defeat.

The Hall of Mirrors was laid out like a cathedral, though they had forgotten to include an altar. The aide-de-camp handed us over to a senior officer, who in turn led us to Clémenceau. As we approached the big official table, my apprehension grew. I felt like a man who takes his place in the orchestra pit knowing he cannot read a single note of music.

Clémenceau was the first to see us. Our wounds and

our awkwardness marked us out. The Prime Minister advanced towards us and shook our hands. Above the din, I heard him say: 'I want them to see and know.' Then, addressing us directly: 'It's clear you were in a bad spot.' A tear ran from the corner of his eye.

We were placed on the side, like choristers at Sunday mass, directly opposite the German delegation, who were unable to ignore us. The signing ceremony was a lengthy one. I had to nudge Weil with my elbow twice to stop him falling asleep. It was a great day, and I came away convinced that this had indeed been the war to end all wars.

The newspapers all agreed – the terms imposed on the Germans on that fine June day in 1919 ensured that war was now a thing of the past.

My uncle was insistent that I should stay at his house for longer, but I decided to go back to my apartment in October – although I agreed to spend the weekends at Nogent, sure that I would always find a warm welcome from my cousins. My mother and sister had already returned to the Périgord, where time was starting to weigh heavily on my grandfather.

Old Nallet, who had heard that I wanted my old job back, summoned me in November. He was almost apologetic that he had not been present at my interview with Grichard. He had been in the Somme at the time, trying in vain to find the remains of his son, who had vanished in the marshes during the winter of 1916. The war had taken his child from him, and as if that were not enough, it had denied him a burial place that would have brought his child closer to him.

He was expecting me at the beginning of December. We could work out the exact details of my work later.

And so I found myself back in my apartment, with its ghosts.

Weil, keeping faith with his first love found a job in a plane factory. His one obsession was to fly again. The factory was near Le Bourget, and he slept there during the week, returning to his parents' house near Montmartre on Saturday nights.

We regularly spent those Saturday nights in the neighbourhood bars, downing long pints of beer and smoking English cigarettes.

Penanster had returned to his manor house in Brittany. I had suspected him of wanting to join the Franciscans and retreat from the world, but for the moment, he was hard at work setting up an association whose aim was to unite and help our comrades who had lost their faces. Weil thought that his generosity would win out over the temptation to be a recluse. Penanster often wrote to us. We could sense how much he enjoyed writing. To him, it was one of the clearest demonstrations of friendship. Weil and I did not feel quite the same, but although we could not always reciprocate, he did not hold it against us. His warm, friendly letters continued to arrive regularly. He was running his estate, and although it did not yield an enormous amount, it allowed him to survive.

It was the beginning of a period when we were very much in demand by the War Ministry, which regularly sent us invitations to plays and operettas and concerts. There were seats specially set aside for us in every place of entertainment in Paris. We formed a show within the show. It was hard to miss our bandaged faces in the auditorium, and during the interval everyone would turn to look at us. Some people were only just discovering how terrible the war had really been. Sometimes, in the silence, you could hear the wheezing of one of our comrades, his insides damaged by poison gas.

I was starting to appreciate music, and whenever there was a choice between a comic opera and a concert, I would choose the concert.

On 14 December, I attended a performance of Fauré's Requiem at the Théâtre des Champs Elysées. Weil had declined the invitation, and there were only two of us occupying the seats reserved for the war wounded. I recognized my neighbour, who was to my knowledge the only man to have lost both ears simultaneously in an explosion. We had shared the same ward during the summer of '17. I whispered a few words to him, without expecting a reply – I remembered that he had also lost the power of speech. Despite everything, he managed to smile and to show me how happy he was to see me again. I asked him for his address, informing him of Penanster's proposed association and hoping that he would take advantage of it. He scribbled it on a little piece of paper and added, at the bottom of the page: 'We got them, didn't we?' My only response was to squeeze his arm very hard.

Then the music enveloped us.

I loved that Requiem. It made me cry – not with the kind of tears that overcome you in public at some unexpected emotion, nor with those private tears that make you sink deeper into your lonely misery. No, these tears came from a combination of two things – the best that mankind can produce and the memory of the horrors that had almost led the human race to ruin.

And there she was.

Her face suddenly appeared to me, like the prow of a ship just before a tragic collision. Her perfect profile seemed to float in the light, and her eyes glowed with colours that I had never forgotten.

I felt madness beckoning. I recalled the tragic story of Penanster's mother. I had thought, up until then, that I was managing to put up an almost spirited resistance to fate, but my mind was not robust enough to confront the reality of this woman, who was more beautiful than ever now that she had reached maturity.

If I had believed in God, I would have begged Him to take my life there and then. I put my head on my companion's shoulder. He thought I had been taken ill, and wanted to get help, but I took his hand and assured him that I was fine. I made my way through the crowd to the exit. I had felt her eyes rest on me as I stood up, before they returned to the orchestra with the same nonchalance I had observed five years earlier. I clearly did not remind her of anything, except that the war had left behind some walking debris.

I stood outside in the pouring rain for a while, smoking one cigarette after another. When the packet was completely empty, I returned to the entrance. The concert had nearly finished. I went off to find a taxi and asked the driver to wait for me. I peered questioningly at all the women coming out of the theatre, frightening them with my dislocated face looming out of the night.

When she finally appeared, she was on the arm of a man the same age as me.

He was a distinguished-looking man, clearly from a good family, but Clémence seemed to find him a little over-eager in his attentiveness to her, though she was too polite to reject him outright. He was courting her, which must mean she was free. It seemed that the man wanted her to go somewhere with him, but she had made up her mind not to go.

I found the studied elegance and refinement of the man – a man who had never had to suffer – unbearable, as was this seemingly interminable game of seduction.

Just as my hatred was about to get the better of me, Clémence dismissed her suitor with a gesture of the hand, the kind that women use when they want to cut things short. The man walked her to a taxi that was parked a few metres from the one I had reserved.

I got into my cab and ordered the driver not to let the other one out of his sight, no matter what. It was a matter of life and death. Seeing that there was a woman in the picture, he replied that he couldn't promise anything, and that he had no wish to be involved in an accident. I promised him a tidy sum if he managed to keep up with the other car, and a bullet in the head – on my word as an officer – if he lost it. The man, who seemed too young to have been in the war, took my threat quite seriously, and bent low over the wheel, as if to urge his car forward.

The chase lasted nearly ten minutes, under a deluge of melted snow. The taxi finally stopped in the place de Breteuil. Clémence got out and disappeared into an impressive-looking building. I kept my eyes on the windows, in the hope of seeing a light come on. But none did, which must mean that her apartment was at the back of the building. What matter? I knew her address now, and that was enough.

On the edge of the square, almost facing the entrance to her building, was a little bench, the seat of wood and the framework of iron. I sat there all Saturday and Sunday morning. Saturday was another snowy day, between Christmas and the New Year. Big flakes were falling, heavy with water, but I made my way through them until I reached what was to become my observation post. I had wrapped myself in a big woollen overcoat, with my face hidden in a scarf.

The hours passed and she did not appear. But the occupants of her building noticed my presence and grew anxious at the sight of a man sitting motionless in the snow, possibly freezing to death. In order not to attract any more attention, I left my post, frustrated and annoyed. I was plagued with anxiety. Perhaps she had only been passing through and would not come there again for months. Or perhaps she was sick and confined to her bed. Or perhaps she had simply left for the provinces.

That evening, as I did every Saturday, I joined Weil at our usual bistro. He was in an exceptionally good mood, but when he saw how subdued I was, he started to get worried. He was afraid I was falling into one of those depressions which were a real threat to all seriously wounded men, and which were still leading some to take their own lives. I reassured him on that point.

'So what's going on? I've known you for four and a half years, and I've never seen you like this!'

'A woman.'

'A woman! Are you crazy, or what? Adrien, you're my friend, I know what you feel, and I'll be blunt. It's a luxury you can't afford. You have to stop right now. If you don't, you're just letting yourself in for a lot of heartache. Shall I tell you what love is, for people like us? It's like having someone take hold of your guts and unroll them. Imagine how pleasant that must be! Talk to Penanster, he'll tell you the same thing. You're just like a soldier during the Nivelle offensive – you don't stand a chance.'

'It's a long story. It's more complicated than that, and stop talking to me about butchery.'

'Calm down. We'll order a good bottle of Cahors, shall we? And let's see what's on the menu. Oh, look, tripe. It would be tripe, wouldn't it? All right, tell me all about it, I promise I shan't lecture.'

So I told him the whole story, feeling as I did so that I was recounting a dream.

'And what are you going to do?' he asked, when I had finished.

'Watch her without her seeing me.'

'You know what that's called, don't you?'

'Seeing without being seen, you mean?'

'Yes. It's called voyeurism. Or else plain insanity.'

'All right, then – I'll talk to her.'

'And tell her what?'

'That I love her.'

'And you think that having last seen you in full possession of your faculties, with a handsome face and all the prestige of a future hero, she's going to rush into your arms? Forget her, I beg you. The woman doesn't even deserve you.'

'I thought you weren't going to lecture me.'

'I don't want you to suffer. It's still too early for that. There are so many things to do. As a matter of fact, I have a proposition for you. I'd like us to get together to build a new plane. A plane for carrying mail. Or goods. A big biplane. I've made a model. Why not come to my house tomorrow, and I'll show it to you.'

'Tomorrow? I can't.'

'Lunch with the family?'

'No, a date.'

'With that woman?'

'We have a date, even though she doesn't know it.'

'Adrien, you're off your head.'

'I'll speak to her if it kills me.'

By Sunday morning, the snow had started to fall again with big, thick, clinging flakes, muffling the atmosphere and covering my bench with a layer of cotton wool. I was at my post by seven in the morning, so as to be sure not to miss her. Two hours passed. My mouth was dry from the cigarettes I was chain-smoking. I decided to enter the building. I went in with head held high, straight past the concierge, whose face was pressed to the window.

She sprang out of her *loge* like a jack-in-the-box.

'Are you looking for something?'

'I have an appointment with a lady,' I replied, with the most perfect composure.

'What lady?'

'A tall lady with blonde hair.'

'Don't you know her name?'

'What does her name matter? I know who she is.'

'And what time is your appointment?'

'Five years ago.'

'Are you pulling my leg?'

'Do I look like someone who pulls people's legs?'

A glance at my face convinced her of the contrary.

'All right,' she said. 'Stay there, if that's what you want.'

I had been sitting on the bottom steps of the staircase for a good three quarters of an hour when a little girl came hurtling down the stairs and stopped a few metres from me. She must have been four or five. It had been years since I had been face to face with a child. We had fought the war for the sake of the children, but I knew so little about them. Sensing my embarrassment, the little girl began to move with a strange, cautious slowness. With her big inquisitive eyes and her smart Sunday clothes, she impressed me. She stopped when she was one step above me.

'Did they hurt you?' she asked, tilting her head slightly.

'Yes, a little.'

'Was it the Germans?'

'Yes.'

'But now they've gone.'

'They've gone.'

'Forever?'

Before I had time to reply, a young woman had joined her and taken her hand.

She nodded to me in greeting, then pulled the little girl away. The girl could not take her eyes off my face, as if it were a page from a book that children were not normally allowed to read.

Another woman was coming slowly down the stairs. Before she appeared, I heard the sound of her voice calling to the first woman, whom I took to be the child's governess. I recognized that voice as if I had known it all my life. The young governess and the child were already walking in the snow. I was standing facing the stairs, and for some reason I put my hands together when she reached the bottom steps.

'You're late,' I said in a low voice, as she was preparing to pass me.

She did not appear offended, nor particularly surprised. 'Who are you?'

'The first time I spoke to you, madame, you didn't have the strength to turn me away. The circumstances were not quite the same as now, I admit, but perhaps you'll allow me to take the same liberty again?'

She reflected for a brief moment, her eyes fixed on the marble of the entrance. 'We met before the war, didn't we?'

'I believe we shared the last night of peace.'

Her face lit up for a few seconds, before reality rushed in to darken it. 'Adrien?'

'Yes, it's me, though I admit the outside may not be quite what it was.'

She remained silent for several long seconds.

'If I'd known, I . . .'

'Oh, we didn't lack for anything. We were well looked after. It's just that after that night, I had begun to think that . . . They brought me your letter in the hospital. It was clear enough, it did not leave me much hope, not even an address. I've thought about you a lot in the past five years.'

'How did you find me?'

'The Fauré Requiem. I saw you half-turned from me, and you saw me, too, without seeing me. That's a strange thing about the disfigured. People notice them, can't avoid seeing them, and at the same time don't see them at all. I've been following you since then, stalking you like a hunter – or a maniac. I wanted you to know that, despite appearances, I'm still the same.'

'I'm so sorry. If only I'd known . . .'

'There is no room for guilt or commiseration.'

As I looked at her standing there, so beautiful, with the light from the staircase behind her, and her skin so white, the years rolled back and I was overwhelmed by memories.

'What happened to your pianist, the one who was responsible for our first meeting?'

'He's dead.'

'It's my turn to be sorry.'

'He died of penumonia at the front, in the early winter of 'fourteen.'

Something strange suddenly occurred to me. That little girl hopping from foot to foot in the clinging snow . . . I couldn't see any way of raising the subject without risking offending Clémence.

She did not ask me the slightest question about my wound, and it was much better that way.

We walked a few steps in the snow, preceded by the little girl and her governess. A long silence fell between us.

I asked her how old her daughter was.

It wasn't the real question, but she gave me the real answer.

'She was born in August 'fifteen. It's not your blood that flows in her veins.'

The dream had only lasted a few moments.

'I would have given a lot for her to be a link between us,' I continued in a flat voice.

'She isn't.'

The little girl turned and ran to her mother.

'Do you know this man?'

'Yes, I know him, but go back to Mademoiselle Lormot.'

The little girl smiled at me, then hopped back to her governess.

Clémence seemed overcome with emotion, and I said as much to her.

'I'd like so much for you to forgive me.'

'Forgive you for what? It wasn't you who fired that shell. Besides, you had already abandoned me before I was wounded. So there is nothing to feel sorry about. And surgery is making enormous strides. For example, take a friend of mine who was wounded in the face in the last weeks of fighting. They cut a piece out of his skull and grafted a rib onto his forehead. You can hardly see his wound any more. Perhaps one day I'll get back the face you liked so much . . .'

'I'd like us to remain friends.'

'Yes, why not give the dog a bone?'

Seeing the pained look on her face, I immediately regretted what I had said.

'I'm sorry, I didn't mean to hurt you. What I meant was that I have nothing left in my life except fragments, crumbs of satisfaction. Not quite enough to live on yet. Sometimes, to fill the gaps, I resort to mockery. To be honest, I don't know if I want to be your friend. We were never friends before. I have three friends now – two men and one woman, who've been through the same sufferings and humiliations as I have. We're a sort of club. We may argue from time to time, but nothing will ever tear us apart, that I know for sure.'

The pavement was slippery with snow, and she leaned on my arm.

'I must confess something to you,' she said. 'After my daughter's father died, I tried to get in touch with you again. In March 'fifteen, to be precise, I sent a friend to you with a letter. I had told him all about you, and that I wanted to see you again. I wasn't sure of the address. I didn't even remember your surname. But I remembered which floor it was. He took the letter, but did he find the right place? I suppose not, or you would have mentioned that you'd received it.'

'I didn't get back to my apartment until May this year. I searched every centimetre in the hope of finding a letter from you. There was none.'

She gave me an embarrassed smile, and then was lost in thought again.

'And what did you write in that letter?'

'I simply apologized for the note I had left and gave you the address where you have now found me.'

'Couldn't you get used to being alone?'

'I simply wanted to see you again, to feel the same attraction I'd felt for you before.'

'All I can offer you now is repulsion, I'm afraid.'

'Haven't you been hurt enough, that you must try to hurt yourself?'

'We survivors know that we are condemned to a certain . . . realism, let's say. Man is a creature of flesh and blood. When our blood has flowed and our flesh has been twisted so that we're changed out of all recognition, we have to resign ourselves to living on simple things and avoid any impulse that would end by reminding us what we've become in reality. That's why I accept your friendship. Out of realism.'

'So we *will* see each other again?'

'I suppose so . . .'

I AM no historian, and have no intention of becoming one. Just because you have been intimately connected with a period does not mean that you can claim to grasp its substance, even after many years. But I would like to take the liberty of putting a date, if not to an event, then to the beginning of a period, a period when France allowed fear to overcome her and started searching for scapegoats. It seems to me that this attitude, so opposed to the character of the 'men of '14', began to gain the upper hand in the nineteen twenties.

Even children had changed. I remember a day when a dozen of them, sitting in a square, began to laugh at me, and even pretended to throw stones at me. In all the years since the war, we had aroused pity, compassion, often embarrassment – but never the fear that makes people want to defend themselves against anyone who disturbs them.

In 1924, I got married.

She was just nineteen, and I was nearly thirty-four. She was a schoolfriend of my youngest cousin. She had a curious Polish name, Skowronek, and at the beginning of our relationship I teased her about her name, telling her it sounded as if you didn't so much say it as sneeze it. She was constantly asking my cousin about me. To her, I was a hero, and she was always very kind to me. Above all, she took the time to listen to me, even though I spoke so slowly. I spent hours telling her about my years at Val de Grâce, and she really enjoyed it. She did not talk much about herself, but I learned from my cousin that her father had been a tailor, a Polish Jew, who had settled in France at the beginning of the century, and her mother had been an excessively pretty young woman.

The tailor had died in the floods of 1910, and the mother had wasted no time in placing her daughter in a boarding school.

I realized that this small, frail young girl was in fact strong and energetic. And when I asked her to marry me, I had proof that she was also brave.

Our wedding was a joyous occasion. My best friends were there – Marguerite, Penanster and Weil – as well as others who had shared my years of confinement at Val de Grâce.

On such occasions, our little community radiated a joy in life that surprised those who still had their whole mouths to laugh with. We drank, ate and smoked more than we should. But above all, we had that feeling of extreme freedom which is the prerogative of those who no longer need to care about their image and who derive from their proximity to death and their daily cohabitation with suffering a kind of detachment from all the things that make men so limited and petty. It was rare for two disfigured men to meet without exchanging a spicy story or a rude joke. Our good humour impressed those around us, and we influenced them with our appetite for the present.

I was the first severely disfigured man to find a wife, which created a great wave of hope among my companions. After all those years, I was getting back into the swim of normal life, that everyday life so often decried by those who do not realize how happy they are.

The most extraordinary thing was that in the years that followed, all my companions ended up getting married. All except Marguerite, because she was a woman, and a disfigured women is something the world cannot deal with. As her sole reward for devoting her life to helping other people, Marguerite was destined to remain alone until her dying day.

The day after our wedding, life played another bad trick on one of us. Penanster took the night train for Brest. Early in the morning, looking for the toilet, he mistakingly opened the door leading off the train. He was found lying on the tracks in his pyjamas, with several fractured ribs. As soon as we learned of his accident, Marguerite, who was on leave from her job at the ministry, where she was in charge of the provision of prostheses for war veterans, rushed to him to offer our support. I soon joined her, as did Weil a few days later. We could no longer bear the thought of one of us being in hospital alone.

The year 1926 was another happy year. Penanster married at the end of spring, and Weil followed quickly at the beginning of summer. My wife gave birth to a baby girl at the end of June. As Penanster said, showing us his good profile and speaking with that inimitable loftiness of his: 'We have entered a great period of normalization.'

The birth of my daughter gave me a sweet sense of euphoria. Unlikely as it may once have seemed, my existence would continue after me. My deep joy followed nine months of worry, not to say anguish. I had been afraid my daughter would be born with a deformed face. Luckily, nature paid no heed to the ramblings of my imagination.

This was a period of remarkable advances in plastic surgery. Several times, I was offered the chance to undergo new skin or cartilage grafts. I was promised a more pleasant face. I don't think it was because I feared the pain of further operations – or the persistent smell of ether – that I refused the offers. This face was mine from now on, it was part of my story.

Penanster lived mostly on the private income from the land he owned in Brittany. Apart from that, his invalidity pension and an inheritance sufficed for his needs.

Although I never had the opportunity to see any of his works from that period, I knew that Penanster devoted a lot of time to painting. Whenever he was asked what style he painted in, he would grin and say 'morbid expressionism'. I understood what he meant much later when I came across a painting by Otto Dix, a German war veteran who had painted terrifying facial disfigurements, based on his memories of the trenches.

Weil developed his plane engine business with the help of his wife.

Marguerite, after her hours at the ministry, worked in a home for the insane, men whose reason had been destroyed by fear in the trenches. Unable to interest other people in her, she devoted her life to serving them, but she never became fanatical about her altruism, a failing that affected so many and that always alienated me.

Clémence finally married a lawyer who entered politics. He was a good twenty years older than her, which gave me a kind of satisfaction.

Afraid that our relationship might disturb the tranquillity of my family life, I had not seen her since our encounter in the snow.

It was not until '28 that I saw her again, by chance, during a demonstration of war veterans at which her husband gave a short but forceful speech.

She was standing near me. The light rain that fell seemed to flow over her hair without making it wet. It was to be our last conversation.

She gently chided me for my silence of nearly nine years. I tried to explain that I had met my wife soon after, which wasn't entirely true, and that, in view of the circumstances, it had been difficult for me to see her again. Her reply hit me like a second wound, almost as devastating as the first.

'If you had come back to me then, as I thought we'd

agreed when we parted, I don't think this orator would have taken your place.'

The thirties were a strange period. While France sank deeper into crisis and gloom, we invalids held more and more parties, at which we danced and played cards, and drank more than we ate – chewing was still a problem for many of us. What we had in common was a wish to live in the present as intensely as possible, and to be together as much as possible, surrounded by the families we had never expected to have. Our parties always ended up with cards. The children would spend whole afternoons watching the games over our shoulders through clouds of smoke – we always chain-smoked. Our little community radiated a self-assurance and a gaiety that became widely known. It only needed two or three of us to attend a first communion or a wedding for the party to be transformed by these men who feared nothing because they had nothing to lose. Our detachment impressed everyone. We were taken for wise men.

It may have been our isolation and the comfort of our card games, well lubricated with drink as they were, that blinded us to the beginnings of war. We did not want to think it possible. All that we had endured, we had done because we had been persuaded that our war was the last. My friends and I had turned a deaf ear to the sound of jackboots. When Daladier returned from Munich, we thought it had all been settled. The Germans would never dare attack us. Even when they invaded Poland, we continued to believe that peace could somehow be saved.

In the spring of '40, we all left as a family for the north of Brittany. The Germans entered France in May and threw the English army back into the sea, while our own was scattered on the roads. But then Marshal Pétain stepped in and peace was restored. A good peace for those who wanted to believe in it, including us. We had no reason to doubt the good faith of the victor of Verdun. Then the old man started to go off the rails, and capitulation became collaboration.

Weil and I returned to Paris in the autumn, leaving our wives and children in Brittany, under Penanster's protection.

In the train taking us to the Gare Montparnasse, the faces of the people were a picture of fear and suspicion. I realized that France was living through a double tragedy – the biggest military defeat in living memory and the beginnings of a civil war between the puppets of an army of occupation and those who would soon remember our past sacrifices.

Coming out of the station, I felt sick and had to cling very hard to Weil's arm to stop myself from falling. The first time I had seen Germans was the day the treaty of Versailles was signed, which was supposed to ensure peace forever. I had not seen any in Brittany after the defeat. But here they were, in Paris.

The metro was packed. Not a seat to be had. We stood pressed against each other in the noise and heat. Suddenly two German officers stood up from the *strapontins* on which they had been sitting, and offered us their seats. One of them even gave us a military salute.

The gallantry of the victors made my blood run cold, and I forced Weil to get off at the next station.

I put my affairs in order, then went to my office to find out what needed to be done. When I was informed that there was a good chance the company, along with its engineers, would be taken over by the Germans, I decided to collect my savings and return to Brittany to wait for better days.

Penanster kept us going on his income, the size of which he shrewdly managed to hide from the occupying forces. We spent the whole war in Lanloup, between Paimpol and Brehec.

Weil came to fetch his family at the beginning of the winter of '41 to take them back to Paris. He needed his wife's help to continue running his little business, which had also been taken over. He wrote to us regularly. His letters were like him, full of that old detachment, that distance from events, which protected him. All the same, they worried us more and more. It was a long time before he mentioned what he himself called 'the Jewish question', and when he did, he sounded like a journalist, limiting himself to the facts. Exposures, slogans on shops, harassment, the yellow star . . .

His last letter, dated May '42, ended in a sentence only he could have written:

'My dear friends, I like to think that all this fuss has nothing to do with me personally, or my family. I don't see how they could go for a man – or the family of a man – who had his face flattened for France to such an extent that he no longer even possesses the very thing that is supposed to be the mark of the villain.'

Marguerite had a close cousin who worked in the Paris prefecture. At the beginning of June, he informed her that something was brewing. Marguerite wrote to us in Brittany to tell us how worried she was.

I can still see Penanster coming through the little door of our stone house one drizzly morning, sitting down in the dining room, and telling me while I made him a sort of coffee:

'Adrien, you must get ready to go to Paris with me. We have to get the Weils out before it's too late.'

To be honest, I had never imagined that anti-Semitism could lead to death. And when Penanster mentioned camps, I have to admit I thought he was simply exaggerating. I imagined camps of civilian prisoners, but nothing more. But then Penanster confided in me that he was working for British intelligence, and that one of his contacts had confirmed that the Germans were indeed taking the Jews to their deaths.

Clearly the time for discussion was over.

The expedition was organized for the beginning of July. It was not an easy matter getting out of Paris. A Breton police functionary, with whom Penanster was in touch, took Weil, his wife and two children in his car, as far as Maintenon. From there, we managed to get them across France to the West.

Penanster installed the Weils in the cellar of an old agricultural building on the edge of the forest. They did not come out until two years later, at the Liberation.

During those two years, we resumed our habits. Every day, Penanster and I joined Weil for a game of cards. 'Five plus two,' Weil liked to repeat. 'That makes seven years' imprisonment. Not bad for a man who's done nothing wrong, is it?'

One morning in the summer of '44, Ernestine, Penanster's old maidservant, the only one to share with us the secret of Weil's hiding place, lifted the trapdoor covered with hay and announced in a flat voice, without the least emotion:

'The war is over, ladies and gentlemen, and the Germans are out.'

Weil threw his last card on the table and stood up. He was laughing wildly and weeping at the same time, so much so that he almost choked. For several minutes, he could not say a word. When he was finally able to speak, he cried:

'The war to end war!'

We all joined in the laughter. This was the end of seven years of isolation. It had been like a strange play in two acts, one set in the ward of a military hospital and the second in the cellar of a Breton barn.

SINCE the end of the war, Penanster had been suffering from dizziness, blackouts and lapses of memory, all brought on by his wounds. In the spring of 1946, he left for a pilgrimage in the Vercors with a Resistance group. One evening after dinner, he left the little hotel on the plateau where the group was staying, for an after-dinner walk. By the following morning, he had not returned. That evening, he was found in the brambles at the foot of a precipice, dead. In his hands he was holding a monogrammed handkerchief. The blood found on it, as well as the injuries to his knees, indicated that he had fallen several times in his wanderings. Drawn perhaps by distant lights, like the lights of Breton lifeboats, he had ended up in a ravine.

We gave him a superb funeral at the church of Saint-Louis des-Invalides.

Weil and I stood to the right of the coffin, facing the nave. Marguerite, prostrate with grief, sat in the front row. The old comrades arrived one after the other. When they were all seated, a group of young men came in. Some had bandages around their heads. Others had their wounds exposed to the air. Many of them were pilots. They all looked young. They advanced, intimidated by the old ones. There was a lot of sadness in their eyes.

I leaned towards Weil.

'What are we going to do now?' I asked.

He was silent for a long time.

'We're going to teach them how to enjoy life,' he said.

F
DUG

Dugain, Marc.

The officers' ward.

NOV 0 4 2002

$21.00

DATE			